She'd blo

She'd lost h...   ok
at the provo...   he
matter with the man? He was attracted to
her—she had sensed that—yet he persisted in
parading views he must know she didn't hold
with. It would have been much better to stay
cool and deal with his archaic views in a light,
bantering way. And she probably would have
if the wretch didn't attract her so much. Why
was that? She'd never gone in for the strong,
silent type before. Come to think of it, she'd
never met a man like Mike before...

Drusilla Douglas qualified as a physiotherapist and worked happily in hospitals both north and south of the border until parental frailty obliged her to quit. When free to resume her career, she soon discovered that she had missed the boat promotion-wise. Having by then begun to dabble in romantic fiction, she worked part-time for a while at both her writing and physio, but these days considers herself more the novelist.

Recent titles by the same author:

DOCTORS IN DOUBT
CRISIS IN CALLASAY
RIVALS FOR A SURGEON

DOCTORS IN CONFLICT

BY
DRUSILLA DOUGLAS

MILLS & BOON

DID YOU PURCHASE THIS BOOK WITHOUT A COVER?

If you did, you should be aware it is **stolen property** as it was reported *unsold and destroyed* by a retailer. Neither the author nor the publisher has received any payment for this book.

All the characters in this book have no existence outside the imagination of the author, and have no relation whatsoever to anyone bearing the same name or names. They are not even distantly inspired by any individual known or unknown to the author, and all the incidents are pure invention.

All Rights Reserved including the right of reproduction in whole or in part in any form. This edition is published by arrangement with Harlequin Enterprises II B.V. The text of this publication or any part thereof may not be reproduced or transmitted in any form or by any means, electronic or mechanical, including photocopying, recording, storage in an information retrieval system, or otherwise, without the written permission of the publisher.

This book is sold subject to the condition that it shall not, by way of trade or otherwise, be lent, resold, hired out or otherwise circulated without the prior consent of the publisher in any form of binding or cover other than that in which it is published and without a similar condition including this condition being imposed on the subsequent purchaser.

MILLS & BOON and MILLS & BOON with the Rose Device are registered trademarks of the publisher.

*First published in Great Britain 1999
Harlequin Mills & Boon Limited,
Eton House, 18-24 Paradise Road, Richmond, Surrey TW9 1SR*

© Drusilla Douglas 1999

ISBN 0 263 81891 8

*Set in Times Roman 10½ on 12 pt.
03-9912-51382-D*

*Printed and bound in Spain
by Litografia Rosés S.A., Barcelona*

CHAPTER ONE

'I DON'T KNOW,' said Dr Catriona MacFarlane to anybody who asked, when she returned home to Edinburgh after the interview. 'It seemed to go all right, but there were three others on the short list, so I honestly don't know.

'And I'll not mind too much if I don't get the job,' she added for insurance. 'I do want a change from Edinburgh, but I didn't much care for Salchester. It may be England's second city, but it's still a great, sprawling, ugly place.'

'Yona, why do you always have to make the best of everything?' asked her best friend. 'Why not bang on about sex discrimination or anti-Scots feelings—like any normal person?'

'You call that normal?' asked Yona with a chuckle. 'I'd rather believe that Professor Burnley will choose the one he thinks will be best for the job.'

'Is that a fact?' queried her friend. 'Then how come you think that any job you've got so far is all down to being your father's daughter?'

'I do not,' denied Yona, 'but there's a sight too many folk who do. That's one reason for getting right away—to prove that I can make good on my own.' Her other reason—the recent defection of her long-time boyfriend—she'd be keeping to herself.

'I wouldn't have your principles for the world,' sighed the friend. 'Too damned inconvenient by half.'

'Decision time,' said the same friend a week later, when the letter came, offering Yona the appointment. 'You'll turn it down, of course—Salchester being such a ghastly place.'

'Oh, come on!' Yona laughed. 'Surely you guessed I was only hedging my bets. Of course I'm going to accept! It's much too good a chance to turn down.'

'If you say so—but don't say I didn't warn you,' returned Yona's friend, who believed in having the last word.

So the new job was accepted. Goodbyes were said to family and friends and four weeks later, on a wet and windy Monday morning in March, Yona MacFarlane parked her car for a second time in the deplorably rutted and ill-kept staff car park at Salchester Royal Infirmary. Full of hope and anticipation, she made a dash for the department of Rheumatology.

'Are you new?' asked the receptionist of the tall, slender, chestnut-haired girl with the arresting periwinkle-blue eyes who approached her desk.

'You could say that,' said Yona with a smile. 'I'm Dr MacFarlane, Professor Burnley's new registrar. He is expecting me.'

The girl looked rather embarrassed as she said, 'I'm sorry—but I thought you'd be older. The thing is, he's in a meeting, but Mrs Lee, his secretary, said to put you in his room and let her know. This way, please.'

'Would you not like some proof of identity?' asked Yona, as her guide seemed about to leave her alone.

She got a look of surprise for that. 'Oh, no, that's all right, Doctor. If you weren't who you say, you wouldn't know you were supposed to be coming today, would you? Mrs Lee won't be long.'

'It's good to know I look honest as well as young,' murmured Yona, glancing round her new boss's consulting room. It was much like any other, with the standard examination couch, tray of instruments, impressive array of textbooks and a solid-looking desk stacked with paperwork. A sheet of paper, headed 'Southern General Hospital,

Edinburgh' caught her eye. Could that possibly be one of her references?

Yona was bending over the desk, wrestling with the temptation to find out what had been said about her, when a deep male voice demanded roughly, 'And what do you think you're doing?'

She spun round, flushing with vexation at having been caught with her hand in the till, so to speak. Her gaze connected with a large white shirt-clad chest, then travelled up a good twelve inches, before meeting deep-set searching brown-to-hazel eyes in a tanned and rugged face.

The man looked strong and capable and, with his sleeves rolled up to the elbow, she took him for a tradesman, here to mend a faulty windowcatch or something. 'I might ask you the same thing—bursting in like that without knocking,' she reproved him.

He looked thunderstruck. 'I work here!' he exclaimed.

'So do I,' Yona retorted evenly.

'Doing what?' asked the man, clearly sceptical.

Yona was furious with herself for blushing guiltily again. 'What ever Professor Burnley decides,' she said frostily. 'I'm his new registrar.' That's fairly taken you aback, she realised with satisfaction, watching his face.

'I should have guessed,' he said gruffly after a moment. 'Except that before I went on holiday the word was that you wouldn't be here before the beginning of April.'

If he'd been on holiday, that probably explained the tan, if nothing else. 'And now may I know who you are?' Yona asked coolly.

'Mike Preston, orthopaedic consultant. I do most of this unit's reconstruction surgery so I suppose we'll be seeing a fair bit of one another.' He didn't sound exactly overjoyed at the prospect. 'Where is Ted anyway?'

'Professor Burnley is in a meeting, I'm told. Would you like me to give him a message?'

'No—there's nothing urgent. Thanks all the same, Dr MacPherson.'

'MacFarlane,' she corrected as he turned to go.

'I knew it was something like that,' said Mike Preston as he closed the door.

Yona barely had time to decide that there was one new colleague she wasn't going to like before a small, plump blonde came bursting into the room. 'Remember me, Dr MacFarlane? I'm Sharon Lee. The professor hopes his meeting will be short, but meanwhile here's an outline of your orientation programme for you to look over while you're waiting. Would you like a coffee?' She seemed so anxious to please that Yona accepted, although it wasn't yet half past nine.

Sharon Lee rushed off to see about the coffee and Yona sat down to read, relieved to see that she wasn't being thrown in at the deep end. They were giving her time to get the feel of the place by sitting in on clinics and lectures, visiting the laboratory where the research was going on and, of course, ward rounds.

There was even the option of going to Theatre to see the rugged Mr Preston in action, but Yona resolved to pass on that if she could. Unfortunate first impressions apart, she'd never much liked the surgical side of things.

She thanked the girl who brought her coffee and was making a note of the dates and times of her own teaching sessions with students of the various disciplines when Professor Burnley came in, full of apologies for not being there to greet her on arrival.

'They do it on purpose, you know—these administrators.' He sighed. 'Fixing meetings at a moment's notice is their way of showing us who's in charge. Changed days since my great-grandfather's time here. Did you know there's been a Burnley at Salchester Royal Infirmary for four generations? Good journey down?' he asked before Yona could comment. 'And have you found somewhere decent to stay?'

Yona said 'Imagine' to his first question, 'Fast and uneventful' to the second and that she was putting up at the hotel she'd stayed at for her interview to the third. 'Just while I look round for a flat,' she explained.

'Sharon will be able to help you there,' he said. 'Her husband is an estate agent.' He then fixed Yona with a serious look. 'Before we go any further, I'd like you to know that I'm delighted you've decided to join us. The name MacFarlane is not unknown in medical circles.'

Yona hoped he wasn't aware of her dismay. Please, not another job secured on her father's reputation... 'Thank you, sir,' she managed. 'I was very pleased to have been selected.'

'Everybody happy, then,' he summed up. 'Now, let's keep it that way by getting up to the wards. Thursday is my usual day for a full ward round, but I thought a quick dash round now would be the quickest way for you to get acquainted with patients and staff.'

Sister Evans had been off duty the day of the interviews, but her senior staff nurse, who had showed the candidates round, had hinted at a dragon first class so Yona was prepared for the searching scrutiny she received.

'I run a very tight ship, Doctor,' warned the dragon when the prof had made the introductions.

'I'm very glad to hear it, Sister,' Yona responded crisply.

Sister eyed her suspiciously, as though wondering whether the new girl was being cheeky, decided to reserve judgement and turned away to tell the professor that everything was ready for his inspection.

'When is it not?' he asked, getting a slight smile and a queenly nod for his trouble.

They started in the women's ward, where Yona felt at home at once. Just as in Edinburgh, most of the patients were in their middle years and being treated for acute episodes of rheumatoid arthritis. However, since the incidence of rheumatoid arthritis was two or three times higher in females, it was no surprise to find a wider range of rheumatic disease among the male patients.

Without needing to refer to the notes, Professor Burnley gave Yona clear and concise accounts of the first few patients. Then they came to the bedside of a thin, pale young man in his early twenties.

'Can you remember when you first noticed trouble with your back?' asked the boss.

'Well, there was the accident at work last year, Doctor, but before that I was often stiff in the mornings—especially in wet weather.'

'Of which we get far too much in Salchester,' observed the prof. 'Any ideas, Dr MacFarlane?'

Yona had already noticed the man's poor chest expansion. 'I'd be thinking in terms of ankylosing spondylitis, sir,' she said quietly. Never alarm the patient unnecessarily.

'So far, so good. Now take a look at his X-rays.'

Yona did so and was unsurprised to find tell-tale changes in the sacro-iliac joints.

'Is there anything else you'd be looking for?' wondered the boss.

'I'd check his peripheral joints, of course, although the incidence of such involvement is low. I'd be looking particularly at his eyes, though.'

'Why is Dr MacFarlane interested in our patient's eyes?' Professor Burnley demanded of the trembling houseman, who mumbled that he didn't know.

The professor then went into overdrive, delivering a mini-lecture on the incidence of iritis in this condition. 'Have you taken any blood samples yet?' he wound up.

'Oh, yes, sir—this morning, sir.'

'And what do you think the blood will tell us?' That question came next, when the little group had moved out of earshot of the patient.

'Whether he's anaemic, sir?' suggested the hapless houseman.

'We are looking at ankylosing spondylitis, not rheumatoid arthritis,' reproved the professor. 'We shall probably find little more than a raised ESR. What's the significance of that?'

'Infection, sir.'

'I prefer to say evidence of abnormal pathological activity in this case,' said his superior. 'How long have you been with us now?'

'A week, sir.'

'Hmm! Well, I suggest that you sit in on as many of Dr MacFarlane's clinics as you can, which shouldn't be difficult. This is a very easy number for house officers, compared with the acute general medical wards.' As they left the ward, he spun round to demand of Sister, 'Has Mr Carpenter been to look at our Felty's syndrome spleen yet?'

'I assume that Mr Carpenter is a general surgeon,' whispered Yona to the senior house officer, Dr Price, who had been hovering protectively at her side all the way round.

'That's right,' he whispered back, 'though Mike Preston reckons he ought to be an orthopod with a name like that. Mr Preston is the orthopaedic surgeon who works most closely with us,' he added.

'I've met him,' said Yona in a toneless voice, earning herself a speculative sideways glance.

The houseman had caught up on her other side to ask,

'Please, Dr MacFarlane, why is the spleen so important in Felt's syndrome?'

'Felty's, after the doctor who first described it,' she corrected automatically, before going on to describe a rare syndrome in which rheumatoid arthritis is complicated by lymphatic problems and enlargement of the spleen. 'And, if I were you, I'd make time to read up on all the rheumatic diseases before the next round,' she advised.

'I'm only here locuming for a month until I can get on Chests,' he grumbled.

'Well, don't let the boss hear you say that,' she advised. 'Besides, there's no such thing as too much knowledge in our profession,' she pointed out as they caught up with the rest of the procession.

'You've soon settled in,' murmured Dr Price, looking impressed.

'One rheumatic unit is much like another,' claimed Yona. 'More or less,' she added. There'd been nobody like the rugged Mr Preston on the Edinburgh unit.

'No operation required for the moment, then,' observed the professor when he'd read Mr Carpenter's report on the last patient to be seen. 'So, what shall we do for this lady, Dr MacFarlane?'

'There may well be a case for ACTH,' Yona answered guardedly, in case he was setting a little trap for her.

When he beamed approval, she knew she'd been right about the trap. He then went on to explain to the bemused houseman the different uses for the various types of steroids. But he was well behindhand, thanks to that surprise early morning meeting, and he had to complete the round without any more testing questions for his new registrar. 'And now, Doctor, you're down to visit our research laboratory, if my memory serves me correctly,' he said.

Yona agreed, but Sister Evans intervened. 'Those personnel people have rung, asking to see Dr MacFarlane at noon,' she said, revealing her own thinking on the newfangled human resources jargon.

'How inconvenient,' said the boss with a sigh. 'Never mind—best get it over with before you start work. One-thirty in Outpatients, then,' he went on. 'Dr Price will take you to lunch, won't you, Charlie? I'd take you myself, but I have to show a party of visitors from Bolivia round the department.' He was away before anybody could delay him further.

'Does the professor always operate flat out like he did this morning?' Yona asked her immediate junior, when he'd told her how to find the staff canteen via Admin.

'Almost always, but this morning there was the extra incentive of impressing you, I guess.'

'Because I'm new and he wants to set me an example,' she assumed.

'Because he admires your famous father,' corrected Charlie. 'He was ever so chuffed when he found out whose daughter you are. Here, have I said the wrong thing?' he asked as her brows drew together in a frown.

'No, of course not,' she denied quickly, because he looked so crestfallen. 'It's just that I'd hoped I'd got this job on my own merits and not because my father has made a name for himself in medicine.'

'And I'm sure you did,' he said earnestly. 'I'm nearly sure he never found out until after he'd made up his mind to offer you the job.'

'I hope you're right,' she said with equal earnestness. 'It's so galling to be thought of as just Daddy's girl when you've been qualified and working hard for six years.'

His eyes widened. 'Six years? You must have been an infant prodigy, then.'

'And you must have taken a charm course,' she riposted.

'Good lord! Is that the Admin block? It looks more like a five-star hotel.'

'As befits the most important bit of the whole hospital,' he said satirically. 'See you later, then, quean—as we call pretty girls around her.'

After completing the paperwork relevant to her appointment, Yona was surprised to be ushered into the office of the assistant chief administrator, Medical Division, for what turned out to be a pep talk. Team spirit was the thing, Yona was told, something that seemed to consist of keeping Admin personally informed of every decision, large or small. Yona was then told how lucky she was to have been chosen for a post in Salchester Royal Infirmary.

'Oh, I realise that,' she returned firmly. 'Professor Burnley is very highly regarded throughout the medical profession.'

'You misunderstand me,' said the ACAMD, looking nettled. 'We don't go in for personality cults here. Our philosophy is that every member of staff is of equal importance.'

I'll bet! thought Yona. Aloud she said, 'Certainly the front-line troops need their back-up staff—if you'll forgive the military analogy—but a hospital without its doctors and nurses would make a nonsense of most other departments, would it not?' Yes, that found its mark, judging by your expression! 'But I'm afraid I'm keeping you from your lunch. Thank you for taking the time to talk to me—I found it very informative.'

I was probably way over the top there, decided Yona after the woman had told her rather shakily that she was free to go. But what a nerve she's got—lecturing me as though I were a potential trainee stamp-licker straight from school!

'You didn't enjoy that little session,' commented Charlie

Price when Yona eventually joined him in the canteen, after taking two wrong turnings.

She smiled and gave him a potted version of the interview, and was soothed by his indignation. 'I dare say she meant well,' she felt able to say then. 'And no doubt she has a relevant health-care qualification.'

'Are you kidding?' asked Charlie. 'She came to us from a firm of management consultants that had gone bust.'

At that, Yona burst out laughing, drawing interested glances from nearby tables. Charlie seized that chance to make some introductions. What a pleasant lot, she thought later when going to join the boss as instructed. And a vast improvement on Mr Michael Preston!

She was five minutes early, but the professor was already there, eating a stale-looking sandwich and drinking coffee from a paper cup. 'You've caught me,' he said, looking like a naughty schoolboy. 'But my wife has threatened to leave me if I miss lunch more than twice a week.'

'I'm surprised that she allows you even two weekly lapses,' returned Yona, who was warming rapidly to her new boss. 'I do hope it'll not be long before you let me take some of the load off your shoulders, sir.'

'You must be a very formal lot up there in Edinburgh,' he said, 'if registrars are still calling the consultants 'sir'. Some of the younger ones here get their first names—even from students sometimes, though I'm bound to say I find that just a trifle too egalitarian.'

Yona recalled Charlie calling Mr Preston Mike before she said, 'I was brought up the old way—sir.'

'Yes, you would be,' he replied. Was that another reference to her famous father? She hoped not. 'Anyway, behind the scenes I'm Ted,' he invited.

'Thank you—and I'm Yona,' she was saying when brisk, firm steps in the corridor were followed by a single brief rap on the door before Mike Preston came in. He had added a tie and a white coat to his morning outfit but, in Yona's opinion, he still didn't look the part.

'I hope you don't mind, Ted,' he began, without so much as a glance for Yona, 'but I've told Senga Taggart that she can come this afternoon. She can't manage the usual follow-up clinic. Her niece is getting married that day.'

'No problem,' agreed the professor, 'and it will be nice for our new colleague to meet up with a fellow Scot,' he added, by way of bringing Yona into the picture. 'You've not yet met my new registrar, Mike—Mr Mike Preston—Dr Yona MacFarlane.'

'We met this morning—briefly,' said Mike Preston. He didn't add that he'd caught her trying to read something on her boss's desk, as she'd been prepared for. Yona was grudgingly grateful for that. 'You'll find us Lancastrians very direct and down-to-earth after the rarefied atmosphere of Edinburgh, Dr MacFarland,' he warned.

MacFarland, indeed! She'd show him. 'We Scots are a hardy lot, Mr Prescot,' she retorted, chin well up. 'It'll be our dreadful weather, no doubt.'

His eyes narrowed at that and the merest twitch at the corner of his mouth suggested that he'd recognised a worthy adversary. Meanwhile, the professor, who hadn't noticed the name mis-calling, was welcoming their first patient.

Mrs Brown had walked in slowly and painfully with the aid of elbow crutches. She wore a supporting brace on her right knee and, in the absence of a nurse, Yona helped her onto the examination couch and took off the brace, revealing a thickened, swollen knee stuck in about twenty degrees of flexion.

'You'd make an excellent nurse, Doctor,' Mike Preston

murmured satirically as Yona resumed her place to one side to give the consultants room.

'They teach attention to detail in rarefied Edinburgh,' she murmured back, but he gave no sign of having heard that. He was already palpating the patient's knee with sure and gentle hands.

After the examination, he said gently, 'I'm very sorry if that was painful, Mrs Brown.' Then he studied the X-rays, before saying to Ted, 'No doubt about it—a replacement is the only answer.' Speaking to the patient again, he went on, 'You do realise, I hope, that replacing your knee joint is not an instant cure? There'll be weeks of hard work with the physios before you're really mobile again.'

'I'm not afraid of hard work, Doctor,' Mrs Brown said hardily. 'If I had been, happen I'd not have worn my bones out scrubbing. But I'll be damn glad to get rid of the pain—if you'll excuse the language.'

He smiled at her in a friendly way Yona hadn't supposed him capable of. 'Professor Burnley tells me you've already made a good start by losing some weight, so I'm sure you'll do just fine. I'll put your name on the list and get you in as soon as I can. I'm sorry I can't give you a definite date, but accidents and emergencies play havoc with our waiting lists.'

'Get me fixed up before Wakes Week, and that'll do me,' Mrs Brown responded cheerfully when Yona had replaced her support and helped her to stand up.

'Please, what is Wakes Week?' asked Yona when the patient had gone.

'A throwback to the days of the Lancashire cotton mills,' explained Ted. 'They all used to shut down for the same week in July, and the towns were totally quiet, with all who could afford it going off to places like Blackpool and Morecambe. Is there nothing like that in Scotland?'

'Oh, yes! In Glasgow, they still talk about the Fair Fortnight—also in July. In bygone days, the shipyard workers would go 'doon the watter'—that is, down the Clyde on the steamers to all the little seaside resorts.'

'Trust the Scots to go one better and have two weeks off,' observed Mike Preston.

'Yes, superiority will out,' returned Yona smoothly.

Ted said he hoped he wasn't going to have a rerun of Bannockburn on his hands and how about getting in the next patient?

Five more potential candidates for surgery came and went, all receiving the same meticulous assessment. 'How often are these clinics held?' asked Yona while they were waiting for the famous Senga Taggart.

'Once a month,' both consultants said together.

'Why?' asked Mike.

'I was thinking that if they were any more frequent, you must have a very long waiting list. However—'

'I have,' he said. 'I get plenty of direct referrals from GPs as well.' He was looking at his watch and frowning. 'Surely Senga should be here by now? I'm due in Theatre in fifteen minutes. I wonder what can have—?' He broke off when a thunderous knock on the door was promptly followed by the lady herself.

She was obviously a great favourite with both men. 'It's good to see you after so long, Senga,' said Ted.

'And looking so well, too.' That was Mike's contribution.

She accepted that as no less than her due and and asked, before either of them could introduce Yona, 'So, who's the lassie, then?'

Ted did the honours. 'Meet our new colleague, Dr MacFarlane. She's a fellow countrywoman of yours.'

'Is that so?' she responded. 'Then she'll be richt guid at her job. Whaur are ye from, hen?'

'I'm Edinburgh born and bred, Mrs Taggart,' said Yona with a smile.

'I'm frae Glasgow myself,' responded Senga with a definite air of one-upmanship. 'Have ye telt them the auld saying yet, Doctor?'

'Not yet, but I can guess the one you mean.' Yona turned to the men. 'If you were to drop in around teatime in Glasgow, they'd say, "I'll just put on the kettle," but in Edinburgh they'd say, "You'll have had your tea." Or so it's said…'

'Aye, that's the one, though I'm bound to say I've met some real nice Edinburgh folk in my time,' Senga confided, causing chuckles all round.

'But I've no' come here just for a blether,' she said reprovingly. 'You'll be wanting to know how I'm tholing your latest bit of handiwork, Mr P. Well, it's just fine. See?' She stretched and bent her elbow several times. 'I'm full o' spare parts he's put in,' she told Yona. 'He's awful clever, ye ken—for a Sassenach,' she added provocatively.

'Any more of your cheek and I'll send you back to Glasgow for the next new bit you need,' Mike threatened good-humouredly. 'But, while you're here, I suppose we'd better check you over.'

Yona stood by and watched, thinking what a good team these two men made—even if they had forgotten her for the moment.

When Senga Taggart left, Mike went with her without another glance in Yona's direction. She was surprised at the strength of her resentment.

'Well, that concludes the first part,' said Ted. 'And now we've got…' he counted the folders '…six new patients, and four of them referred as query rheumatoid arthritis.' He paused. 'Something we know everything about except the cause, despite all the theories flying around. I'll just carry on as usual if that's all right with you, Yona, but just you butt in if there's anything you want to ask,' he invited as he pressed the buzzer on his desk.

In the space of the next three hours six patients came and went—and all of them were as obviously impressed by Professor Burnley's painstaking approach as Yona was.

'Now, then, tell me how what you've seen so far today compares with what you're used to,' he commanded when the clinic was over.

'Would you think I was dodging the issue if I said it feels just like home?' she asked.

'Not at all—I'd be flattered. Go on.'

'From the small sample of both in- and outpatients I've seen, the incidence of rheumatoid arthritis appears similar—as are your treatment methods.'

'It's good to have one's regime endorsed from such a source,' he said, but worrying her again if only he'd known it. But he probably meant Edinburgh in general and not her father in particular. Dr MacFarlane senior was an eminent neurologist.

'I was very impressed by the way you picked up that dermato-myocitis two patients back,' he was saying.

'Were you really?' she asked, surprised. 'I thought it was pretty obvious.'

'To the specialist observer maybe—but the GP had failed to spot it.'

'Is that so surprising?' she asked. 'It must be horrendous to be in general practice and never know what weird disorder is coming through your door next. At least in hospital we're sticking to the same kind of disorder—most of the time anyway.'

'That's very true,' he agreed. 'You're a bright girl, Yona

MacFarlane, and I can see you're going to be a great asset to the team.' He glanced at the clock. 'Not quite six, so an early finish for once,' he said. 'I'll do the letters for this lot while it's all fresh in my mind, but you may as well take yourself off now. I hope today hasn't been too confusing for you.'

'Heavens no! I've enjoyed every minute. Good evening then, Ted—and thank you for making my first day so pleasant and easy.'

'The pleasure was mutual,' he assured her.

Pleasant and easy, she thought, going to get her car. That wasn't completely true, was it? I have a feeling I'm going to have to watch my step with that man Preston…

CHAPTER TWO

ON YONA'S third morning at Salchester Royal Infirmary, Sharon Lee came into her consulting room and laid a bulky package on her desk. 'Details of a few flats in decent districts fairly nearby,' she explained. 'I can get you some more if there's nothing suitable.'

By then the first clinic patient was being ushered in so, with a smile of thanks, Yona laid it aside. She also smiled at the patient, but got a frown in return. 'I always see Dr Redmond,' said the patient, a determined-looking woman in her mid-fifties.

Yona explained that Dr Redmond had left and she had taken his place.

'All this chopping and changing is very upsetting.'

'Dr Redmond was here for almost three years,' said Yona.

'And I've been coming for seven,' she was told.

There was no answer to that, so Yona asked whether the short-wave diathermy and exercises, prescribed on her last visit, had been beneficial.'

Mrs Ribble said it certainly kept her going, but she needed another doctor's line to carry on with it.

'I shall have to examine your knees first,' said Yona firmly, and was told that Dr Redmond always trusted her.

Wisely Yona decided to ignore that and insisted on being allowed to see for herself. The left knee was quiescent, but the right one was very red, shiny and swollen. 'I'd say you've recently given this a bit of a bash, Mrs Ribble,' she said, earning a glance of grudging respect.

'So I'm definitely needing the treatment, then.'

'No, Mrs Ribble. I'm going to draw the fluid off, bandage it firmly and send you home with some elbow crutches to rest up for a week.'

'Oh, nice,' said Mrs Ribble. 'It's easy seen you don't live on the seventeenth floor on your own and never getting out.'

She wasn't the first patient Yona had had whose only diversion was a trip to the hospital for treatment, but there were other remedies—like lunch clubs and day centres. When she'd dealt with the knee, Yona asked the nurse to make sure that Mrs Ribble saw a medical social worker before getting the ambulance home. 'And I'll be seeing you again this day week,' she explained.

'I suppose you're doing your best.' The reply was grudging.

The patients that morning were mostly arthritic, with roughly equal numbers having either osteoarthritis, often described as 'wear and tear', or rheumatoid arthritis, with all its associated symptoms. Mrs Kavanagh was one of the latter. 'I can hardly drag myself round these days, I'm that tired, Doctor.' She sighed as she eased herself into the patient's chair.

There was no need to look at her eyes to see that she was very anaemic. 'I've been taking the iron tablets, honestly,' said the patient, guessing what was in Yona's mind.

'I'm going to suggest iron injections instead,' said Yona, 'and I'm also going to take some blood, even though you say your joints are quiet just now.' Because if I'm not much mistaken, you're boiling up for an acute attack, she thought, before asking what other medication Mrs Kavanagh was taking.

Mrs Kavanagh said she was taking just the aspirin as the chloroquine upset her stomach.

Yona had never met that before, but no chloroquine or other controlling drug explained a lot. 'You must come and see me again next week when I've got the results of today's blood tests,' she said firmly. 'Then we'll know what other medicine to try.' If we don't have to bring you into the ward for the full works...

There were several other patients Yona needed to see again the following week and the chief appointments clerk took her to task over it. 'You're disrupting my figures,' she complained.

'I'm sorry, but all those patients really need to attend,' said Yona wearily. She'd been on duty for the whole medical block the previous night and had been too busy to do more than catnap occasionally in an armchair. Also, she was getting a headache.

'You're new here, Doctor, so I'd better explain that your function is just to check them over now and again and refer them to their GPs for any treatment.'

'If that was all that was required, then there'd be no need for them to come here at all,' said Yona, trying to keep her temper. 'But I'll tell the professor what I've done this morning and let him decide if I was right or wrong.' The phone rang and Yona picked it up. 'But now you'll have to excuse me. Sister Evans has a problem and needs my help.'

It was a bold person who would rate her claim for attention higher than Sister Evans's, and the clerk went away without another word.

Sister was waiting for Yona in the main corridor of the unit, and greeted her with 'We have just admitted a woman for assessment who, to my mind, has a fractured neck of femur.'

'Did she fall?' Yona asked quickly.

'She says not and I believe her, but as she's been on steroids for many years...'

'I get the picture,' said Yona grimly. Steroids were a boon until the side-effects caught up with you. 'Let's go and take a look.'

'We must get her X-rayed for the orthopods,' she said when she'd examined the patient, who had the tell-tale signs of fixed outward rotation and muscle spasm round the hip joint, 'but you were quite right, Sister. What a good thing you called me so promptly.'

There was nothing that Sister liked more than being told that she was quite right. She preened and said, 'But I'm afraid this unfortunate episode has put paid to your lunch, Doctor, as you're due in Theatre at one-thirty.' She always knew everything. 'I'll get you some coffee and send down to the canteen for sandwiches, if you like.'

Yona wasn't the least bit hungry so she said, 'Please don't bother, Sister. Just some coffee will be fine.' Then she sank thankfully onto the nearest chair, feeling quite ashamed of herself. A busy night on call had never affected her like this before. I must be getting old, she thought wryly.

Sister's coffee was as strong and bracing as herself and just what was needed to see Yona through a long afternoon of standing under the heat and brilliance of the theatre lights. This afternoon would be almost the last stage of her orientation programme and the bit she'd been looking forward to the least, and the fact that it was Mike Preston who'd be operating was an added irritation.

Yona had done her best to be pleasant on the few occasions their paths had crossed so far, but they were only too obviously on different wavelengths.

'More coffee, Doctor?' Sister was asking.

'No, thanks—that fairly hit the spot and I really must be

making a move. They tell me that Mr Preston is a stickler for punctuality.'

'Mr Preston is a perfectionist who expects perfection from others,' Sister returned with such obvious approval that Yona was left feeling quite depressed.

She'd been sure that Mike Preston would ask her a lot of questions in an attempt to catch her out, so she'd taken care to read up on joint replacements. When he seemed content just to keep her at his elbow and describe procedure in detail as he worked, Yona felt irritation rather than relief. What a waste of an evening! Another black mark against him.

He was swift and sure and very neat—she had to admit that—but more than once she felt herself swaying in the heat as the afternoon wore on.

Only one more case now—a hip replacement for severe osteoarthrosis—and Yona reckoned she could just about last out. It was the squelching and scrunching as Mike dislocated the hip, prior to replacing the damaged head of femur, that did it. With a tiny mewing sound, like a distressed kitten, Yona slipped unconscious to the floor.

She came round in the surgeons' rest room under the kindly and interested eye of the theatre nurse manager. She flushed scarlet with embarrassment as she realised what had happened and she poured out a stumbling apology.

'Think nothing of it,' the man said soothingly. 'It happens more often than you'd think to somebody unused to the heat and the atmosphere. Particularly if they're coming down with the flu.'

'But I'm not! At least...' Her head was throbbing and she ached all over, as well as feeling hot and cold at once.

He slipped a thermometer under her tongue. 'Just as I thought,' he said a moment later. 'Thirty-nine and a bit. Now tell me you're not getting the flu, Doctor.'

Yona smiled weakly and told him she wouldn't dare. 'I can't stay here, though. I must be dreadfully in the way...' But when she tried to stand up, she collapsed back on the couch.

'Nonsense,' said the man bracingly. 'The theatre team will be some time yet and by then I'll have fixed up for somebody to drive you home.'

He handed her two white tablets and a glass of water. 'What are these?' asked Yona suspiciously.

'Aspirin,' said a nurse, laughing. 'Still the best thing for flu, as I'm sure you agree. I've things to do now, but there's a bell at your elbow if you want anything.'

The only thing that Yona wanted was to be out of this place where she'd made such a fool of herself before Mike Preston came out of Theatre. Her head felt clearer now and the next time she got to her feet she managed to stay upright.

'Would you please tell the nurse in charge thank you very much, but Dr MacFarlane feels fine now and has gone to Outpatients?' she asked the first nurse she saw. The main door of the theatre suite clanged shut behind her a second after Mike stepped into the corridor.

Phew! That was a close thing, but a miss was as good as the mile it had seemed, plodding down that corridor from the rest room. Now, which way to Outpatients? She hadn't quite finished the morning's notes when Sister Evans sent for her.

By the time Yona was ready to leave, the evening rush hour had begun and she didn't feel up to coping with the traffic. It was raining heavily, though, so she'd need to get her brolly from the car. No sense in drowning while she waited for a taxi.

She was head and shoulders in the car, and feeling about for her umbrella in the fast fading light, when she heard

Mike Preston say in an exasperated voice, 'Haven't you got more sense than to drive when you were out for the count less than an hour since?'

Yona pushed herself out of the car and turned to face him indignantly. 'I was not about to drive off,' she insisted. 'I was merely looking for my umbrella.'

'Oh, yes—then where is it?' he asked disbelievingly.

'Not where it usually is! I must have left it at the hotel.'

'That's as likely as anything else, I suppose,' said her tormentor. 'You'd better lock your car and come with me.'

'Where to?' she asked haughtily, standing her ground.

'I'm offering to take you home—and preferably before we both drown,' he spelt out for her, before seizing her arm and towing her faster than she could cope with across the uneven ground. 'Are you still feeling groggy?' he enquired when she stumbled and he had to hold her up.

'No,' she said untruthfully,' but this car park is an absolute disgrace.'

'For once I can agree with you,' he muttered, unlocking a large VW and virtually lifting her into the front passenger seat.

'I had intended phoning for a taxi,' Yona informed him when he got in beside her.

'You'd be lucky at this time on a wet night,' he returned shortly. 'I suppose you know you've offended the theatre manager—walking out the way you did? He'd gone to a lot of trouble, finding a porter who was free to drive you home!'

'If that's so, then I'm sorry,' said Yona with dignity. 'My only wish was not to cause any more trouble—and I did leave a message for him with a nurse.'

'Which he didn't get,' retorted Mike Preston, sounding rather smug.

Yona bit back a sharp reply and settled her chin into the collar of her coat.

'Did you hear what I said?' he asked after a minute.

'Yes, thank you—I did,' she returned frigidly. 'However, as everything I say to you is wrong—and with all this horrendous traffic for you to cope with—I decided not to...to annoy you any more than I seem to have done already!' A marvellous answer from one so sorely tried, she considered proudly.

His only reply was a sharp indrawn hiss and he didn't speak again until he stopped the car outside her hotel. He said then, 'If you'll take my advice, you'll get an early night.'

'I intend to,' Yona told him quietly. As she opened the car door, she was struck by a sudden thought. 'How did you know where I was staying?'

'Somebody must have mentioned it,' he answered casually. 'Ted, probably. Can you manage?'

'Certainly,' she answered loftily. 'And thank you so much for the lift—it was extremely kind of you.'

She managed to get out all right, but rather spoiled the effect by stumbling on the top step of the hotel as she pushed against the heavy swing door. 'Hateful, hateful man,' she muttered as she went inside.

A surprising number of hospital workers had the curious idea that they themselves were somehow immune to the ills they dealt with daily and Yona was no exception. It was, of course, the heat of the place and her personal distaste for operating theatres which had caused her to pass out that afternoon. A good night's sleep—even though it had been the remedy suggested by that awful man Preston—and she'd be as right as rain.

But after a fitful night of fever, headache and aching

limbs, Yona was forced to admit that the kind theatre manager hadn't been so far off the mark after all. She felt about for the phone on her bedside table and rang in to report sick, feeling very guilty. Doctors weren't supposed to be ill—and certainly not after only three days in a new job.

Her new boss rang her at lunchtime and soon put her right on that score. 'You're crazy,' he said when she told him she'd be in for sure the next day. 'If I were a GP and you were my patient with the flu, I'd sign you off for a week. Keep taking the aspirin and stay in bed for at least forty-eight hours. OK?'

In her weak state, Yona responded gladly to authority and meekly promised to do as she was told.

By Saturday the fever was away and, although her legs felt rather rubbery, her head was clear. She got up, took a leisurely bath and put on jeans and a sweater. She was debating a trip to the hospital to clear her desk when somebody knocked on her door. 'Come in,' she called, expecting the chambermaid.

'I'm Meg Burnley—Ted's wife,' said the plump, merry-eyed brunette who came in. 'I hope you haven't been feeling neglected, but Ted's been up to his eyes and I was working full time this week, which I don't usually. Anyway, I've come to carry you off to our house for the weekend—if you think you can bear it. You don't know anybody down here, do you? So that has to be better than convalescing in an hotel.'

'How wonderfully kind!' exclaimed Yona, who hadn't been looking forward to the next two days. 'If you're quite sure I'll not be a trouble...'

Meg said she'd never heard such nonsense and they'd been intending to ask her for Sunday in any case.

The Burnleys lived in a charming, four-square ex-farmhouse in a pretty village on the northern fringes of the city. By the time they'd returned her to her hotel on Sunday evening, Yona was firm friends with both of them. 'It was worth coming to work down here just to meet you two lovely people,' she told them, getting a farewell hug from both Burnleys for that.

Ted had said he didn't expect to see Yona at work before Wednesday, but she was there as soon as he was next morning. 'I'm quite better,' she insisted when he frowned at her. 'So, please, sir, what would you like me to do?'

'As you're told,' he riposted, 'but, as that's obviously a non-starter, how about running one or two little errands for me? Apart from anything else, it'll help you to learn the layout of the place. But have a word with Sharon first. She wants to know if you saw any flats to your liking on her list.'

While confined to bed, Yona had sifted through Sharon's submissions and one stood out a mile—a two-roomed place with a balcony, on the top floor of a modern service block which overlooked a leafy park and was scarcely five minutes' drive from the hospital. Having arranged to view it that evening after work, she picked up her list of errands.

It was while discussing some unusual findings in a patient's blood samples with the chief biochemist that Yona got her first inkling of a possible cause for Mike Preston's reservations about her.

Their business concluded, Dr Nonie Burke asked the new girl how she was settling in.

By then, Yona was used to that question and she replied that everybody she'd met so far had been amazingly kind and helpful.

From that, Dr Burke promptly assumed that Yona had not yet met Mike Preston.

Ah! thought Yona. She'd heard it said that Nonie Burke

was a fine chemist and an even finer gossip. 'Once or twice,' she said. 'Just briefly. I'm sure he's very—efficient...' She wondered if that was enough to get Nonie going.

It was. 'Of course you know he was dead against your appointment.'

'No, I didn't,' returned Yona, although that had been fairly obvious, come to think of it. 'Is he one of the diehards who don't think medicine is a woman's job?'

'That, too, probably, though I don't know for sure. The thing is, a particular friend of Mike's was one of the applicants, and the guy was absolutely desperate to get the post.'

Yona recalled the other three on the short list—a woman and two men. She wondered which one fitted the bill. 'There was a chap—a worried-looking man rather older than the rest of us. Lewis, I think his name was...'

'That's the one. He and Mike were contemporaries at medical school, but an early marriage, kids one after the other and no peace or spare cash to buy time to study for his membership... Get the picture? Love has ruined more than one promising career,' declared Nonie Burke scornfully. As well as liking to gossip, she was said to drift effortlessly from man to man, always managing to avoid serious involvement.

'It's lucky for me that Mr Preston had no say in the appointment, then,' said Yona.

'His friend stood no chance anyway—not without his MRCP. And with Professor Sir William MacFarlane's daughter on the short list,' declared Nonie bracingly. 'But what's with this Mister stuff? I'd no idea you Scots were so formal. Listen, if there's anything I can do to help you settle in...'

Yona thanked her and said she'd remember that.

Unfortunately, well-meaning Dr Nonie Burke had already done just the opposite, by depressing her on two counts, had she known it!

The wretched thing was that there seemed to be no way of finding out whether her father's worldwide reputation had really played a part in her selection. She would just have to sit it out, while doing her damnedest to prove her worth.

Mike's antipathy might be easier to deal with—now that she knew the cause of it. She was eager for their next encounter, but when would that be?

Thursday morning, and Ted had another of those hated meetings, but he'd left a string of things for Yona to attend to before the ward round.

Two new patients had been admitted the day before— one of Ted's and Yona's own Mrs Kavanagh, seen last week and almost her first patient. As Yona had expected, Mrs Kavanagh was dangerously anaemic so, before giving Ted's patient the once-over, Yona set up a drip for transfusion.

'That is a junior's job, Doctor, so where is Dr Connor?' asked Sister, who had taken a dislike to the houseman.

'Dr Connor is busy with the routine blood samples,' Yona answered patiently, 'and I want this lady to have two pints of whole blood as soon as possible.'

'But, surely, an hour or two,' Sister protested.

'I have no objection to undertaking lowly tasks when the occasion demands,' said Yona in her grandest manner. It had been a pretty good take-off of Sister herself, had she realised it—and probably the reason for Sister retreating in some disarray.

The routine examination of the other new patient came next, so that Yona would be au fait with all the new problems before the group discussion after the round. Then she chased up X-rays and lab reports. By the time she returned to the ward, Ted was ready to start.

The round followed the same pattern as on her first day except that this time Yona knew all the patients. That was just as well because the prof was in what Charlie Price called his Mastermind mood.

'Why isn't Mrs Jacobson wearing her forearm splints, Dr MacFarlane?'

'She's developed some painful nodules over the olecranon processes, sir, so I asked the plaster technician to shorten her splints. I'll reapply them as soon as they come back.'

'I see. It's a pity about the nodules, but it's not surprising—given the severity of her condition.'

'Why the cervical collar for Mrs Baker, Dr MacFarlane?'

'She was complaining of pain last night and when I checked her over I found that her grip was very weak. I've arranged for an X-ray of her cervical spine in case there's some subluxation.'

Yona got an A-plus for that, and another when the boss read her meticulous notes on the new patients. 'You must have been in very early this morning, Doctor,' he commented.

'She was in the ward soon after eight, sir,' Sister Evans put in. 'Before Dr Connor,' she added with a touch of malice.

'If the old dragon had her way, this entire unit would be staffed by women,' whispered Charlie in Yona's ear.

There was no answer to that so Yona pretended she hadn't heard.

'I'm going over to Ortho now to say hello to last week's ops cases,' said the prof when the round was over. 'You may as well come too, Yona.'

He must have sensed her surprise because he added, 'It's not strictly necessary—they're in Mike's excellent care while they're in his wards—but I think they like to know I've not forgotten them.'

'And I'm sure they appreciate the thought,' agreed Yona, warmed by this further proof of his commitment. She'd definitely made the right choice in coming to Salchester.

She felt less sure about that when they found Mike Preston on Orthopaedics. 'Ted—good to see you,' he said first, and then to Yona with rather less warmth, 'I hope you've recovered from your bout of flu—or whatever it was, Doctor.'

That had sounded as though it had been a bout of self-indulgence he'd suspected, but she was resolved to meet his hostility with all the good humour she could manage. 'Yes, I am, thank you, Mr Preston. And I'm glad of this chance to apologise properly for disrupting your operating session.' The smile that went with that was wasted on him.

'Nobody supposes that you did it on purpose,' he said. 'Strange, though, all the same. It's not as though there's flu going about just now.'

'There was quite a lot of it in Edinburgh when I left,' she recalled. 'I do hope I didn't bring it with me,' she added half-laughingly.

'So do I,' returned Mike, deadpan. 'It'd play havoc with an already critical bed situation.'

Yona's striking blue eyes darkened almost to purple as they always did when she was irritated. She flashed Mike Preston an angry look, before turning to Ted and asking in a voice of honey whether it might not have been wise to put her in quarantine.

He grinned widely and treated her to a friendly pat on the shoulder. 'I'm inclined to leave you on the loose for the present,' he said with a chuckle. 'And if there is an epidemic, I'll take the blame. After all, I was the one who urged you to start work as soon as possible. OK if we say hello to our mutual patients, Mike? I promise not to let Yona breathe on 'em.' He was completely unaware of the tension between the other two.

'Sure, and, as you say, she's your responsibility.'

He nearly said 'problem', thought Yona as she followed her boss in the ward. It's not my fault his friend didn't get the job, so why must he be so unpleasant? What have *I* done—apart from just being here?

She put that problem aside while Ted chatted to and laughed with the shared patients, visibly raising their morale. Then he introduced them to Dr Redmond's successor and Yona said that she was looking forward to seeing them in the follow-up clinic.

'It isn't strictly necessary to make these visits,' Ted repeated as they left the unit, 'but, as I said before, I think they appreciate it.'

'I'm sure of it,' she agreed, her mind still half on Mike Preston and his attitude. 'My father always says that it's the willingness to go that extra mile which marks out the good doctor from the merely competent one.' Damn her unwary tongue! She'd sworn never to quote her father as an authority on anything in this new environment. Mike Preston could take the blame for that!

But Ted was agreeing wholeheartedly. 'Your father is a wise man, as well as an exceptionally clever one,' he said.

At the clinic that afternoon Yona saw Dr Redmond's old cases while Ted took the new patients. The first two were routine, but the third rang some bells.

Mrs Smith had been diagnosed as having rheumatoid arthritis—that was, the definitive sheepcell test had been positive—but today she was complaining most of her sore eyes. 'And it seems like I'm never free of the cold, Doctor.

It's cough, cough, cough all the time and my husband says I'm driving him mad.'

'It can't be much fun for you either,' said Yona, thinking, Honestly! Some men! 'Do you cry much?' she asked.

'Oh, no, Doctor—he's not that bad!' She'd quite misunderstood Yona's question. 'Anyway, I don't think I could cry if I tried. My eyes feel that dry—and my mouth.'

'Just as I expected,' confirmed Yona as she examined Mrs Smith's eyes, finding the tell-tale ulceration of the cornea. 'I'm going to prescribe some special eye drops which you should find comforting.' Then she asked if the patient was taking her chloroquine and aspirin regularly, as prescribed.

'Like clockwork, Doctor,' came the answer. 'I haven't forgotten what a state I was in before I started.'

'That's the ticket! The pharmacy here will give you enough of the eye drops to get you started and I'll write to your GP today so that he'll know what we're giving you when they're finished.' That's only the second case of Sjögren's syndrome I've ever seen, Yona realised as Mrs Smith went out.

She told Ted all about it as they compared notes on the clinic afterwards, while strolling towards the exit. Naturally, he wanted all the details.

'No hair loss or nail changes—just the keratoconjunctivits and dryness of the upper respiratory tract so far, so I hope we can contain it with hydrocortisone eye drops. She's such a dear little woman, Ted! Why is it that only nice folk get ill in this horrible world?'

'Wait until you're my age, Yona,' he advised with a rueful smile. 'I've met a few who asked for all they got— and so will you before you're done with the job.' Then he changed the subject by saying, 'Do you know, I can't remember the last time I finished work before six. I only hope

Meg doesn't have a heart attack when she sees me home at a decent hour for once.'

'Meg doesn't have a cardiac problem, does she?' Yona asked quickly.

'Bless you, no—and I trust she never will. I'd be lost without Meg.'

'I know,' she said impulsively. 'You two are like the two sides of a coin.'

'It's a great piece of luck to find your one and only early in life,' he declared with heart-warming simplicity. 'It saves all those wrong leaps in the wrong direction other people seem to make,' he added whimsically.

'All the men I've felt inclined to leap at so far have preferred their women to be thick as two short planks,' Yona was astounded to hear herself admitting—but, then, Ted, like his wife, was so easy to talk to.

'Then they were the dumb ones—and a sight too dumb to deserve you,' he declared, causing her to laugh aloud.

'That's better,' he said, laughing himself. 'Now, be off home with you while you have the chance of escape.'

'Not before I've been back to the unit to check on Mrs Kavanagh, boss. She was a bit depressed this morning so I promised I would.'

'You're a kind girl,' he told her warmly. 'And kindness in a doctor is as important as skill. Not that you haven't the skill,' he added hastily. 'I wasn't saying that.'

'I'm sure you weren't.' Yona gave him her widest smile and an impulsive pat on the arm. 'Drive safely, now,' she said. 'Salchester's rush-hour traffic is as bad as Edinburgh's—and that's saying something.'

She was turning away, still smiling and thinking how lucky she was in her new boss, when she saw Mike Preston standing in the doorway of his consulting room, frowning. Saw Ted and me laughing together and doesn't approve, she thought. Well, see if I care! 'Good evening, Mr Preston,' she said pleasantly as she passed him.

'Is it?' he asked tersely.

'It is as far as I'm concerned.' She paused.

'I can see that,' he said dryly.

Yes, thinking of his friend and doesn't like to see me on such good terms with Ted. Was this the moment she'd been waiting for to call his bluff?

'On my first day here, you told me that I'd find Lancastrians direct and down-to-earth,' she began firmly. 'That may be true in general, but in your case—I'm sorry, but I really have to say this—I've never met anybody quite so hostile. It's not my fault that I got the job your friend wanted, so why take it out on me?'

She'd definitely taken the wind out of his sails with that. He stared at her for a long and uncomfortable minute, before admitting guardedly, 'I can't deny that David Lewis would have been my choice for the post—and he certainly wouldn't have set tongues wagging, by following his boss everywhere, as you're doing,' he said more fiercely.

'But, then, perhaps you're not aware that Professor Burnley is married,' he had the gall to add, as though excusing the bad behaviour of a silly child.

Never mind purple—Yona's eyes were now practically black with fury. 'Thank you, but I do know that the professor is married,' she told him in a throbbing voice. 'I've been to his house and met his wife. They're both being very kind to a stranger in a strange city—which is a lot more than I can say for some *other* folk I've been so unfortunate as to find myself working with!'

Yona was so steamed up that she marched straight on past the stairs, and had to go to her wards the long way round.

CHAPTER THREE

'I'D TAKE the pasta if I were you, Doctor,' advised the canteen supervisor in a confidential undertone. 'The eggs in that scrambled stuff are not what they seem, if you take my meaning.'

Yona took her advice and added an apple and a cup of coffee to her lunch tray. It was Saturday so the canteen was half-empty.

She chose a corner table, only to discover what an excellent view it gave her of Mike Preston charming a radiographer and the junior sister from Outpatients.

This was Yona's first full weekend on call at Salchester Royal Infirmary, and more than a week since she'd given Mike that dressing down, something which—apart from the relief she got from letting off steam—had done nothing to improve the situation. While perfectly friendly and forthcoming with everybody else, he was as stiff as ever with Yona and people had begun to remark on it.

Ted said simply that he just couldn't understand it, while his secretary, Sharon, had let slip one day that Mr Preston was known to be anti women doctors in senior positions—especially if they were attractive.

Charlie Price's opinion was that Mike fancied Yona—something so unlikely that she'd burst out laughing on the spot. 'You can laugh all you like,' Charlie had said, 'but why else would he watch you all the time when he thinks that nobody is looking?'

'If what you say is true—which I doubt—he's only watching and hoping for me to make a mistake,' declared

Yona. 'He just can't forgive me for getting the job his friend wanted so much.'

But, watching now in her turn, Yona couldn't help being piqued at being the only person in the hospital who wasn't worth a smile. Smiles transformed Mike Preston's strong, rugged face into one of considerable charm and she could see why those two women were hanging on his every word.

Now, if I were like Nonie Burke, I'd flatter him, lead him on, get him hooked—and then dump him, she thought. And that'd damn well serve him right! Except that she didn't believe—didn't want to believe—that Mike Preston could be so easily taken in.

Neither did she believe that he wanted her interest, but he'd got it all the same—just by being so cool and detached. Any girl with a bit of go about her would feel the same, she excused herself on realising that.

Mike had just said something to send his companions into fits of laughter. Yona felt very isolated and alone in her corner and it was a relief when she was bleeped.

Mike glanced up as she hurried towards the door, his eyes narrowing with speculation. Hoping I'll trip over something and go my length, surmised Yona, but when she glanced towards him from the relative cover of the doorway he was laughing with those two again. If he thinks he can freeze me out of this hospital, he can think again, she resolved. I'd stay on even if I hated the place, rather than give him the satisfaction.

She forgot all about Mike Preston when she arrived hot-foot in Accident and Emergency to be confronted with a semi-conscious patient about to go into respiratory failure. Straight into overdrive. 'Endo-tracheal tube—quickly! And an ambubag for hand-ventilating.'

'Gas and air first, Doctor?'

'No time—and she's too far under to feel any discomfort.'

'Oxygen?'

'First let's get this airway established. And somebody stand by with suction. She's all clogged up by the sound of it.'

'That's better,' Yona could say some ten minutes later. 'Now take some blood—her gases must be completely up the spout. Who's the duty anaesthetist? This lady is going to need a ventilator for forty-eight hours at least. No beds, you say, Sister? Don't make me laugh! This is an emergency. Leave it to me—I'll get on to Chests right away. She's probably one of their regulars.' Her patient stabilised for the moment, Yona dashed to the phone.

'Nice figure,' approved a male charge nurse, looking after her.

'And an even better brain,' observed the young house officer who had put out the call. 'Keep your mind on the job, George, and take over the hand-ventilating while I try to get some blood, like the lady said.'

The next call for Yona was less hectic—to an old lady on Orthopaedics with suspected broncho-pneumonia. She had been operated on three days previously for a fractured neck of femur.

'I can't understand it, Doctor,' said a third-year student nurse, both flustered and proud at being left in charge for the first time. 'We've been sitting her out of bed as much as all the others. And the physios have been trying to walk her—only she seems to have forgotten how.'

'I'm sure you've all done everything you could,' soothed Yona, 'but nobody can foresee everything and it says here in her notes that she has a history of respiratory disease. I'll take a look at her and then, if you point me in the direction of her drugs chart, I'll write her up for a broad-spectrum antibiotic.'

'Thank you very much, Doctor,' said the nurse when all that was done. 'I hope you didn't mind me calling you, only all our duty doctors are in Theatre. Besides, this is a medical rather than a surgical condition, isn't it?'

'Quite right,' agreed Yona. 'You did the right thing.'

'Thanks for saying so, Dr MacFarlane. You see, it was the way she was coughing. I was afraid she was going to choke and then when I saw that plug of filthy phlegm— Would you like a cup of tea, Doctor?' She knew she'd got that right at least. Sister always offered tea to visiting medics at weekends—if the ward wasn't busy.

'That's the best offer I've had all day,' claimed Yona, hiding a smile at the girl's timing.

The nurse sped away to get the tea and Yona was writing up her findings when she heard purposeful footsteps she was beginning to recognise. Mike Preston stopped short in the doorway. From the way he was dressed, he had come straight from Theatre. Yona dragged her eyes away from his manly chest. It would never do to let him see how impressed she was.

'And what are you doing here?' he asked bluntly.

'I was called to Mrs Ada White—the fractured neck of femur you pinned and plated a few days ago. She's developed a low-grade broncho-pneumonia and I've prescribed ampicillin four—hourly. I hope you approve,' she added, in a tone that dared him not to.

'Why you?' he asked, ignoring the challenge.

Yona blinked. 'Because all the duty team were in Theatre, and—'

'It would have done when we'd finished. It's quite unnecessary to involve the medical registrar for such a routine problem,' he interrupted censoriously.

'You know that and I know that—but I wasn't going to stamp on a sweet young thing hell-bent on doing her very best,' Yona returned evenly. 'You can tell her off if you want to. That's your privilege!'

'Of course I'm not going to tell her off,' he said, irritated. 'She was only doing what she thought was right for the patient.'

'So was I,' Yona was saying pointedly when the nurse in question came in with a teatray. There were two cups on it. 'Just wondered if you like some tea, too, Mr Preston...'

'Thank you, that was very thoughtful of you, Linda,' said Mike in a completely different tone. 'This is a big day for you, isn't it—your first in charge?'

'Yes, but we've not been very busy so far. About Mrs White...'

'That's all right. Dr MacFarlane has told me all about her. And don't look so worried—this little hiccup was only to be expected with her history, I'm afraid. Is there anything else worrying you?'

'No, thank you—and, as I said, we're not very busy so— Excuse me, please!' She darted out at the sound of a buzzer alarm coming from the patients' loo.

'Are you having tea?' Mike asked Yona as he picked up the teapot.

Does he wish it were a hand grenade? she wondered. 'I was invited and I accepted so, yes, please,' she returned, nettled at the difference between his way of speaking to the nurse and to herself.

Mike filled the cups and pushed one towards Yona, leaving her to help herself to milk. She thanked him and then sat back, determined not to start a conversation that would only lead to another snub.

He surprised her by saying awkwardly after a moment,

'About David Lewis. I don't mind admitting I was hoping he would get your job. He didn't, though—and you did. And, according to Ted, you've made quite a good start.'

Only 'quite'? 'Thank you,' she said coolly.

'So it's probably best if we put a stop to this—this antipathy we seemed to have fallen into,' he went on, as though she hadn't spoken. 'It serves no useful purpose and is rather unprofessional.'

'I couldn't agree more,' she responded, while simmering secretly at the implication that she was the guilty one in this. 'All the same—'

'No post-mortem, please,' he interrupted. 'That would serve no useful purpose either.'

'It might have cleared the air, though,' said Yona, putting down her cup with rather a clatter and standing up. 'But if that's the way you want it...' She went out, leaving her sentence unfinished. The only ending she'd thought of had been smart and cutting, and they'd just decided to be done with all that.

'Hectic weekend, Yona?' asked Ted on Monday morning.

'Par for the course really. Not enough to claim I was rushed off my feet, but the calls were just too frequent for me to leave the hospital in between.' She paused, her eyes bright. 'You'll never guess who I admitted to our unit yesterday!'

'Surprise me,' he invited.

'Our esteemed assistant administrator, Medical Division. She came to Casualty with a sprained ankle and fainted on her way out. I'd just been admitting yet another status asthmaticus—it was quite a weekend for those—so Sister asked me to take a look at her, with her being such a valuable member of staff.'

'Careful, dear, your prejudices are showing,' warned Ted with a broad grin. 'But how come a swooning sprained ankle ended up in a rheumatic unit?'

'The woman was clearly unwell—vaguely feverish, distinctive rash on face and hands, diffuse small bruises which were certainly not due to her recent fall—and when questioned she admitted to fleeting joint pains which she'd put down to having recently taken up badminton.'

Ted's interest had crystallised long before Yona had finished. 'You're thinking of SLE,' he said.

'Yes, so I've sent off samples for ESR and ANF testing, as well as a full white-cell count. She has some early eye symptoms, too. I'll be interested to see what you make of her.'

'The same as you, I shouldn't wonder. And had she never thought of consulting her GP about all this?'

'Yes. She went to see him when she first felt vaguely unwell and he changed her oral contraceptive. Most of her symptoms have shown themselves since then.'

'And how has she taken the news that she's suffering from an ongoing systemic illness?'

'I've left it for you to tell her—once it's certain. Anyway, I think she was rather relieved to have an excuse to lie back and stop trying to cope.'

'If you ask me, it's a very good thing she did sprain her ankle,' said Ted. 'Let's go upstairs and look at her right away.'

'Sorry, Ted,' said Yona, 'but I have to give a group of first-year nurses an introduction to rheumatic diseases, but I wanted to put you in the picture first.'

'Good girl. Off you go, then—but don't blind 'em with too much science at this stage. It might put them off and you know how hard it is to get good nurses.'

'Don't worry—it'll be the Janet and John version for

starters. Did Sharon tell you we've got an extra-big clinic this afternoon?'

'She did—she also told me you're getting the keys of the new flat at the end of the week. Are you excited?'

'Ecstatic,' she claimed as she dashed off. She'd done almost nothing about furnishings and had been hoping to dash down to the shops later on today, but an outsize clinic had certainly put paid to that. I should have gone for something to rent furnished, she was thinking as she hurried round a corner and almost collided with Mike Preston.

He sidestepped smartly and said with the utmost politeness, 'You're in a great hurry, Dr MacFarlane.'

'I'm on my way to lecture to some nurses and I've cut things rather fine.'

'Then, please, don't let me delay you,' he said in the same courteous way, before striding on.

Yona looked after him. She was feeling rather disappointed. From curtness to courtesy had to be an improvement, but it wasn't what she'd been hoping for. But what had she been hoping for? Oh, blast the man and his silly prejudices! She'd waste no more time on him.

Mike Preston was certainly not in the forefront of Yona's mind for some time after that. Ted suggested that she take a couple of days' leave at the end of that week and with Meg's eager help and knowledge of the Salchester shops carpets and curtains were bought, and some small pieces of furniture as well, to supplement what would be coming from Edinburgh the following week.

'You're very wise to get the whole place decorated before you move in,' said Meg on Friday afternoon when they slipped into a coffee-bar to take the weight off their feet.

'And it was wonderful of you to find me that obliging little man who would do it so quickly,' returned Yona. 'I only hope that tomorrow fortnight isn't too soon for my house-warming party, but I'm on call again the weekend after.'

'Of course it's not too soon! Put if off too long and there'll seem little point,' said Meg sagely.

'You always say the right thing,' Yona told her admiringly.

'More by luck than judgement,' claimed Meg. 'And now, if we're quick, there'll just be time to get to Chirk's for the bathroom fittings before they close.'

'Have I really been here four whole weeks?' asked Yona when Ted reminded her that that afternoon's clinic would be a combined one with Mike's.

'Does it seem longer, then?' he asked.

'No—not as long. Let me see now... The first weekend I visited you, the next I went to Liverpool for that symposium, the next on call, this last one shopping with Meg—you're quite right! And I can hardly believe it.'

'Thank you for your vote of confidence,' Ted said solemnly.

'What? Oh, boss, how could you? What I meant was that I can't believe I've been four whole weeks in Salchester. And you know fine that's what I meant!' she was saying firmly when Mike came in.

He looked curious and Ted said serenely, 'My registrar was just giving me a telling off.'

'Was she now?' Mike eyed Yona askance. 'If she were mine, I wouldn't put up with it. How many have we got today?'

'Five,' said Ted. At the same moment Yona said, 'Six.'

'Sorry, five,' she corrected herself. She'd become confused at the idea of belonging to Mike Preston in any capacity. 'I never could count,' she excused herself.

'It's a good thing that you're not Mike's registrar, then.'

Ted chuckled. 'Ortho requires a certain degree of numeracy—with so many toes and fingers to choose from.' He picked up the first folder. 'This is a sad case really, Mike, but it's got its happy side, too. A girl of twenty-five with a twelve-year history of juvenile rheumatoid arthritis who's just got herself engaged and is desperate to walk up the aisle without crutches. But, to do that, she'll need a total hip replacement.'

Yona expected Mike to refuse there and then as hip replacements had a limited lifespan, but he said, 'I did a replacement for a thirty-year-old man only last week, although it was really Hobson's choice. His hip had been shattered in a car crash. Of course, he was hale and hearty before the accident... Still, there's no harm in me taking a look at her. Let's have her in.'

She was very pretty, with soft blonde hair and wide, trusting blue eyes. It was cruel to see her shuffling, old woman's gait and distorted feet in boat-like orthopaedic shoes. And her twisted little hands could only just grasp the upright posts of the forearm crutches she required.

As always, Ted said exactly the right thing. 'You're looking very pretty as usual, Karen. Is that a new necklace?'

She beamed at him with real affection, which was not to be wondered at when he'd been her friend and doctor since she was twelve years old. 'Fancy you noticing,' she said, delighted. 'Roy gave it to me instead of an engagement ring. I mean, who'd want to wear rings on hands like mine?' she asked of Yona.

'Who'd ever notice anything else on somebody with hair like yours?' asked Yona. 'Such a gorgeous colour and beautifully styled. You must give me the name of your hairdresser.'

'No problem.' Karen smiled. 'She's my mum. Her shop's

on the Central Parade.' That was Salchester's foremost shopping mall. 'You'd suit the new executive cut, Doctor.'

'When you girls have finished admiring each other, we should get down to business,' reproved Mike, but with a smile in his voice.

He's quite good at saying the right thing, too, thought Yona. Well, sometimes. To anybody but me...

When Mike had finished examining Karen, he sat down beside her and explained simply and clearly the pros and cons of a hip replacement at such an early age. Relief of pain and increased movement now, to be set against probable reversion to her present state in about fifteen years' time—and with no promises about a second successful operation if her disease didn't go into remission.

But Karen had already made up her mind. 'Thanks for spelling it out, Doctor, but I'll be forty by then so what will it matter?'

'That's me definitely on the scrap heap, then,' said Ted wryly when Karen had gone and they were waiting for the next patient.

'And I've barely got five years to go,' Mike added with a rueful grin. 'Should we book into Sunset House now, d'you think?'

'It used to be said that life begins at forty,' Yona said bracingly. 'Personally, I can't wait.'

Mike eyed her clear-skinned prettiness for a long second and without any apparent admiration, before saying, 'That's too bad—it looks to me as though you've got a long wait.' He'd sounded so daunting that it took her quite a while to realise that he'd actually paid her a compliment.

She hardly had time to feel pleased before a nurse brought in the next patient and said, 'Dr Price has been trying to bleep you, Doctor. One of the new inpatients has just collapsed.'

Yona thanked her, leapt up and darted out. She took the stairs two at a time to reach the bridge that connected Outpatients with the main ward block.

'Most likely a diabetic coma,' she was pronouncing about ten minutes later. 'Has he no history?'

'There is nothing to that effect in the admission notes and somebody will answer for that,' threatened Sister Evans in a voice that spelt doom for poor Chris Connor.

'Not necessarily,' Yona disagreed. 'Occasionally a major episode like this is the first warning.' Hardly ever, in fact, but she wanted Chris to have the benefit of the doubt.

She stayed a long time on the ward, waiting to be sure of her diagnosis, and by the time she returned to Outpatients the clinic was over. When she'd given Ted the details of the latest crisis he said, 'Mike left you a message. He thanks you for the invitation to your house-warming, but as he's on call next weekend he may not be able to come.'

Yona had expected nothing else and she'd only asked him because it would have looked odd to leave him out when she'd asked all her other colleagues.

Ted went on, 'He also said how surprised he was when he realised you'd bought a flat in his block.'

'I've done *what*?' Yona was astounded. She'd left his invitation on the desk in his consulting room because she didn't know where he lived.

'So you didn't know either, then.'

'No, or I'd not have—' She broke off. To say she'd never have bought her flat if she'd known Mike would be a neighbour was just plain silly. Especially as they would probably come and go at different times. Besides, there was more than one entrance so why need they ever bump into one another? 'Are you quite sure you don't mind me taking

Friday off again this week, Ted?' she asked quickly to cover up her apparent confusion.

'How else will you manage to move in, my dear girl?' he asked, but he was wondering what it was that she'd almost said instead.

'Stop fussing,' said Nonie Burke the third time that Yona got up to count glasses and rearrange the canapés.

Nonie was not only a first-rate biochemist and A1 gossip—she had also been a great help in arranging the housewarming. She had produced an old schoolfriend who was now a gourmet party caterer and on good terms with the best cut-price wine merchant in town.

Tonight, Nonie had turned up an hour early, wearing an apron over a shimmering gold silk catsuit because, as she said, if she'd offered her help, a proud stiff-necked Scot like Yona would have pretended she didn't need it.

Yona knew she was fussing. She also knew why, and she didn't like what she knew. For a mature, successful woman of twenty-seven to revert to teenage angst behaviour just because she couldn't get on the right side of one wretched man was pathetic. Yes, you're absolutely pathetic, Catriona Jean MacFarlane, she was telling herself when the doorbell announced the first arrivals.

They were the Burnleys—punctual as promised. Meg had seen the flat before on moving day, but this was Ted's first visit. He strolled round, glass in hand and admiring everything, while Nonie gave Meg the latest hospital gossip.

It wouldn't be a large party—Yona hadn't been long enough in Salchester to acquire many acquaintances. There'd just be the staff from the unit with their partners, Nonie, who was temporarily without one, and Yona's near neighbour Gil Salvesen—if he could get away from the studio in time. Only Sister Evans had declined.

Gil had been quite a find, a raffish, forty-ish, laid-back television producer with a roving eye which had soon homed in on his newest neighbour. He also had a wicked sense of humour and soon had Yona laughing whenever they met. She wasn't the least bit attracted to him.

Guests were invited for drinks at eight, with a buffet supper to follow, so when neither Gil nor Mike Preston had turned up by nine Yona decided not to delay the meal any longer. They were all at the dessert stage by the time Mike appeared. He had come without the partner specified in the invitation and Yona supposed that must be because he was on call. He put a bottle wrapped in fancy paper on the hall table in passing, and said he could only stay a minute.

In the living room he looked round and said, 'I must say this all looks very nice.' It was as though he'd been expecting a shambles.

'I'm so sorry that your friend couldn't come,' said Yona, stung afresh by his attitude.

'Which friend would that be?' he asked, sounding genuinely puzzled.

'I put "and partner" on all my invitations,' she reminded him.

'But I don't have one,' he returned briefly.

'Is there anybody here whom you don't know?' Yona tried next in her best hostessy manner. She wanted to remind him there was supposed to be a truce between them.

Mike looked round again. 'No, I don't think so. You've gone to a lot of trouble,' he said, on noticing the buffet.

Yona saw no reason to tell him she'd employed a caterer. 'Please, help yourself,' she was saying as Gil strolled in.

He knew nobody but Mike and had to be introduced all round, though whether he'd remember so many names was doubtful. Not that it mattered because Nonie latched on to him right away.

'They make a good pair,' said Mike, suddenly appearing at Yona's side some time later.

'Nonie and Gil? Yes, they're very alike in some ways.' She shot him a quick sideways glance under her lashes. 'Kind to strangers, full of life—and great fun.'

He took that personally, as she'd meant him to, but rather than get into an argument she said quickly, 'Please, excuse me—it looks like time for me to go and make some coffee.'

'And it's time I was going,' he said, but he followed her into the kitchen.

'It was good of you to come at all when you're on call,' said Yona, to hide her disappointment at the shortness of his stay. 'And thank you for the present—that was very kind.'

'Routine,' he insisted. Then he asked her abruptly how she liked working at the Royal.

She was surprised. 'Very much, thank you.'

'You're not homesick?' he persisted.

'There's not been much time for that so far. Why do you ask?'

'Meg told me that you knew nobody in Salchester before you came.'

'That's true, but, then, I came to Salchester to further my career.'

'Which is very important to you.'

'Is that bad?' asked Yona, wondering where all this was leading.

'No—of course not. Only most women value their private lives more than their work.'

'Does that not depend on what work they're doing?' she asked, more puzzled than ever. 'I think I enjoy my leisure as much as the next woman, but doctoring isn't like—well, say, doing part-time work in an office or shop for a spot of extra cash. To medicine, you have to give your all—especially if you're a woman. Too many men still secretly see medicine as an all-male preserve.'

'If that was meant personally, let me tell you that I've nothing against women doctors,' he said sharply.

'Really? Then I've been misinformed,' Yona said quietly. She'd had hopes of this conversation when he'd followed her into the kitchen, but they had long since faded.

'So that's why you've been so hostile,' he said.

'*Me*—hostile? Forgive me for asking, but is it not the other way round? I'm not the one whose good friend was pipped at the post for a job.'

He didn't flare up as she'd half expected. 'I thought I'd already made my position clear on that point,' he said quietly. 'I ask you how you like Salchester and whether you're homesick—as I would ask any new colleague—and in return, I get a feminist lecture on sex discrimination. I really don't know why I bother. Nor can I see why the Burnleys and others find you so enchanting!' he added for good measure, before wheeling round to collide with Meg in the doorway. He muttered a hasty apology, told Meg he'd be in touch and left.

'What was that all about?' asked Meg, her eyes bright with speculation.

'I wish I knew,' Yona sighed honestly. 'That man is a closed book to me.'

'Mike? But he's one of the most straightforward men I know!' Meg exclaimed in astonishment.

'I'll have to take your word for that, Meg, dear,' said Yona, 'because he's keeping his good side well hidden from me. But back to basics. I came out here to the kitchen to make the coffee!'

CHAPTER FOUR

'IF I remember correctly, you're on call this coming weekend,' said Ted to Yona as they made their way up to the wards for the weekly round on the Thursday following her house-warming party.

'I was, Ted, but I've changed with my opposite number on Chests.'

'Great! That means you can come to us on Sunday, then. Meg's got a young niece who can't decide between medicine and dentistry and Meg thinks that talking to you might help her to make up her mind.'

'Oh, dear! I'd have loved that, but as soon as he heard I was off, Gil Salvesen offered to show me Lake Windermere.'

'Just make sure that's all he shows you, then,' advised Ted, who hadn't taken to Gil. 'Well, here we are—and, my word, doesn't Sister look fierce today?' he asked in an undertone.

They started as usual on the women's ward, where Mrs Kavanagh had just completed her time on cortisone, intravenous iron and total bedrest and was now, as she put it, raring to go.

Ted said that he was glad to hear it, but a gentle stroll to the bathroom and back, plus the daily exercise class with the physios, would do nicely for the next week or so.

'Mrs Baker wishes to go home,' announced Sister as they moved on to the next patient.

'Out of the question,' said Ted. 'That neck hasn't settled

down yet and I'm not letting her off traction until her neck brace is ready.'

'She's threatening to sign herself out,' declared Sister, who thrived on this sort of thing.

'Why?' Ted asked reasonably.

'She says that Mrs Jacobson's snoring is driving her mad.'

'Then why not put Mrs Jacobson in the side ward if she's keeping the other patients awake?'

'She isn't. Only Mrs Baker has complained.'

'Then put Mrs Baker in the side ward. Really, Sister, I shouldn't have to waste my time on this—it's a nursing problem.' Yona had rarely seen Ted so irritated.

'Mrs Baker is very determined,' warned Sister.

'And so am I,' Ted said grimly.

Mrs Baker was persuaded to accept a bed outside the range of Mrs Jacobson's nocturnal concerts and harmony was restored.

At least it was until they got to the assistant administrator, Medical Division. She'd had the side ward to herself since admission and wasn't pleased to hear that she was to have a room-mate. 'I would have thought, Professor, that someone of my standing in this hospital—'

'You'll be pleased to hear that you may go home tomorrow, Ms Starkey—or this evening if you prefer,' said Ted with a deceptively innocent smile.

That didn't please her either. 'I was counting on staying at least until Tuesday next. I'm having my kitchen redone while I'm in here.'

'Good, that—coming from a disciple of the quick-turnover school,' whispered Charlie Price in Yona's ear. She'd been thinking the very same thing.

Ted had, too, but he was very diplomatic. 'We've diagnosed your problem and established your drugs regime.

That done, it's now in your best interest to leave hospital. What you need is a change of air for your convalescence before returning to your, um, arduous duties.'

'Is there any chance that mine is an industrial illness?'

'Compensationitis, as well as SLE,' Charlie whispered this time.

'Absolutely not,' said Ted, going on to explain that systemic lupus erythematosus was a disease of the immune system and so insidious in onset that she had almost certainly had it for years, before noticing anything much in the way of symptoms. 'I'd say that spraining your ankle was a blessing in disguise,' he wound up.

It took some doing, but Ms Starkey was eventually persuaded that she was well enough to go home.

'I hope they don't all take this long or we'll be here all night,' grumbled Charlie as they moved on.

'You're extremely grumpy today,' teased Yona.

'Pre-exam nerves,' he said. 'I've got my Membership practical tomorrow—or had you forgotten?'

'I'm afraid I had,' she confessed. 'Good luck—I'm sure you'll do brilliantly.'

Ted was asking Sister what they could expect in the men's ward.

'Mr Donkin is still intractably constipated, but we're dealing with it,' she informed him.

'How?' wondered Charlie in a murmur. 'If it really is intractable—'

Yona shushed him as Sister continued, 'And Mr Bowes has some psoriasis on his elbows.'

'I knew it!' said Ted. 'Didn't I say that man was a psoriatic arthropathy? Is it bothering him much, Sister?'

'He says not—he just thought it was dry skin flaking off.'

'I'm very glad to hear it—it must be hellish when it

itches. Did you find time to examine that man transferred from the General this morning, Yona?'

'Yes, I did. I doubt that he's a true rheumatoid, though. He seemed more like a non-specific infective arthritis to me.'

'The sheepcell test will settle that. Why, Dr Connor?' he shot at Chris.

But Chris had learned a lot in the past six weeks. 'Definitive for rheumatoid arthritis, sir.'

'We'll make a doctor of you yet,' joked Ted as they approached the first male patient.

'Can you do me now, Doctor?' drawled a familiar voice from the doorway as Yona sat in her room in Outpatients, doing her letters at the end of the day.

She looked up, astonished to see Gil. 'What on earth are you doing here?' she asked.

'Right at this moment I'm cadging a lift into town,' he said. 'Didn't you tell me you were dashing in after work?'

'Yes, but you shouldn't be here, Gil—really, you shouldn't. How did you get past Reception?'

'I told them I was your lover—what else?'

She couldn't help giggling at that. 'I bet that interested them!'

'They were all madly jealous, let me tell you. Will you be long? Only I've got an appointment.'

'I've just this minute finished—but, Gil, you must promise me never to do this again.'

Predictably, he wondered why not.

'Because—oh, because gentlemen callers are not allowed in the building!'

'Not even a marine would believe that,' he said. 'But for you—anything!'

'Oh, Gil, you are a fool.' She was laughing as they left the building together.

'But you like me,' he said, giving her a squeeze that nearly had them both falling over on the steps.

As bad luck would have it, Mike Preston had parked beside Yona that morning and, of course, he had to be there now, talking to another consultant. 'For heaven's sake, behave and get in quick before he sees you!' hissed Yona, while asking herself why it was so important that Mike shouldn't see her there with Gil.

'Why?' asked Gil, as she might have expected. 'I'm not afraid of him even if you are. Hi, there, Mike,' he called out. 'I've just been discussing a major documentary with your bosses.'

'I can't wait to see it,' Mike called back, looking anything but eager.

Yona was already in the car and was desperate to get away, but Gil reached out and switched off the engine. 'You really must get over your curious fear of that big bear,' he said, sounding quite fatherly. 'You wouldn't want me to think you had a girlish crush on him, would you?'

'Don't be so ridiculous!' she said furiously, starting the car again.

'I'm not so sure it is ridiculous,' said Gil, sounding amused. 'It could be thought very suitable—except that Nonie says he's already fixed up.'

'Nonie is a terrible gossip—and you're even worse!'

'You *do* fancy him,' he challenged just as she backed out much too fast over the uneven, rutted surface. The car lurched as it went over a particularly bad bump, then Yona spun the wheel like a rally driver and shot off towards the exit.

'Hey, steady on, for God's sake—I thought you'd knocked him down then,' breathed Gil, screwing round in his seat to peer backwards over his shoulder. 'No, I think you managed to miss him—at any rate, he's still upright. Just as well—that's no way to get a man!'

'When I need your advice on that subject, I'll ask for it!' retorted Yona through clenched teeth. 'Now shut up and let me concentrate on the traffic!'

'Sister Evans wants to see you in the office when you've got a minute, Dr MacFarlane,' said Staff Nurse the minute Yona stepped onto the unit next morning.

'Now what's wrong?' she wondered aloud.

'Nothing that I know of,' answered the girl, 'but, then, who knows with Sister?'

'Who, indeed?' murmured Yona, resolving to keep the old dragon waiting while she checked with the houseman.

Yona had simmered down overnight, since driving off in such a rage with Gil. She'd hardly known then with whom she was most angry—Gil for teasing her, herself for overreacting or Mike just for being there.

She found young Dr Connor halfway down the men's ward, collecting routine daily blood samples. 'How's it going, Chris?' she asked.

'Not so well as it would if Sister didn't keep ordering me to do something else,' he grumbled.

It wasn't for Sister to order the house officer about. 'What sort of things?' she asked.

'Oh, listen to chests, examine joints that are more than usually painful, help the nurses to lift patients in and out of the bath...'

Par for the course, except the last, but all to be requested—not demanded. 'How many more specimens have you got to collect?' asked Yona.

'I've not started on the women yet, and with Charlie away for his exam—'

'I'll help you,' she said comfortingly, 'and if Sister finds you any more wee jobs before we've finished, just you refer her to me. I dare say she's forgotten that Charlie is off today.'

'And pigs might fly,' sighed Chris.

All the women were enchanted with Yona's efforts. 'Never felt a thing, Doctor.' 'You're ever so quick.' They were only two of the comments.

'Practice makes perfect and, boy, have I had a lot of practice,' she laughed. 'So that's the Dracula act over for the day, girls.' Then she went at last to see what Sister wanted.

When she saw Yona she pushed a tin moneybox across the desk. 'I am collecting for a silver wedding present for the Professor and Mrs Burnley, Doctor,' she said grandly.

'You're in plenty of time—it's not for another six weeks,' said Yona, diving into the pocket of her white coat for her purse and taking out a ten-pound note. 'No, I insist,' she said, when Sister said that was too much from a newcomer. 'They've both been so very kind to me—I don't know what I'd have done without them.'

'The professor and his wife are always kind to new members of staff, Dr MacFarlane,' revealed Sister, in case Yona should think there was anything special about her. The phone rang and Sister picked it up, then said, 'Yes, she's right here, Mrs Lee. No, I'm sure it isn't. I'll tell her.' She replaced the phone, before revealing, 'The professor's secretary has found a folder she knows he wants for his lecture this morning, and she wondered if you'd call in for it on your way to join him.'

'Yes, of course I will. And if there's nothing else, then—'

'No, not at the moment.' Yona was dismissed.

Why does that woman always make me feel as if I'd just

been carpeted? she wondered as she hurried down to Sharon's office.

Sharon handed over a bulky file as she said how much she and her husband had enjoyed Yona's party. Then, before Yona could thank her for her nice little thank-you note, Sharon burst out, 'Isn't it awful about poor Mr Preston?'

'What about him?' asked Yona, her eyebrows raised.

'He had a nasty accident to his foot last evening and now he's in plaster, right up to the knee.'

Accident, last evening, foot, plaster... Yona felt as though she'd been kicked in the stomach by a horse. 'How...unfortunate,' she breathed, only just managing to hide her horror until she got out of the room. She stumbled back to her own room to think.

He'd been right beside her car on the passenger side, so when the car had lurched as she'd backed out so furiously, it hadn't been on account of the rutted ground, as she'd thought, but because she'd run over Mike's foot! Wait, though. Gil had checked and had said that Mike was still upright... Held up by the other consultant, no doubt!

Yona wanted nothing more than to run home and hide, but she couldn't. She had to go and tell her boss how she'd put his friend and a senior colleague in the hospital!

'It's only just round the corner so you'll have no difficulty finding it,' Ted had said confidently when telling Yona the day before how to get to the building where the seminars for GPs were held. Today, though, she was so preoccupied with the horror of having run over Mike's foot that she turned left instead of right as she left the hospital.

Her imagination was in overdrive. She could see the screaming headlines. CONSULTANT SURGEON KNOCKED DOWN BY FURIOUS FEMALE COLLEAGUE. WOMAN DOCTOR RUNS AMOK IN HOSPITAL CAR PARK. Would there be an inquiry? Almost certainly, when the accident had occurred on hospital premises. But where was she? That sign said SALCHESTER WOMEN'S HOSPITAL and Ted hadn't mentioned that. She must be lost.

The first passerby didn't speak English, but the second one pointed her in the right direction. Ted was just about to start his lecture and looked very relieved when Yona hurried in with a whispered apology and put the folder he wanted on the lectern.

Ted was a very good lecturer—clear, concise and gently humorous. The doctors loved it, but Yona only heard about half of what he said. By the time the lecture was over, she'd imagined herself up before the General Medical Council— via the psychiatrist's couch!

When the doctors had all drifted out in search of lunch, Ted said to Yona, 'I hope that gave you some idea of the level to pitch when it's your turn to hold forth. And don't look so scared,' he urged bracingly. 'Just remember that you know a lot more about rheumatology than almost any GP you're likely to meet.'

'You haven't heard,' she said on a dying breath because he wouldn't be treating her as usual if he had.

'Heard what, Yona?'

'About the accident. To M-Mike Preston.'

'I certainly have not! What's happened?' he asked sharply.

'He's got a crushed foot. A c-car ran over it.'

'But that's awful! And you saw it happen, as you're in such a state,' he surmised.

'No, I—' Yona licked dry lips. 'I—did it.'

'You *what*?' Ted was absolutely staggered, as well he might be.

'It was me. I. Gil Salvesen had annoyed me by coming right into my consulting room without knocking and asking for a lift. We had words about that. Mike was parked next to me and gave me such a dirty look, which made me crosser than ever. Then I drove off in a tearing hurry—over his foot. Apparently.'

'What do you mean—"apparently"?' Ted asked faintly.

'Well, the car gave this awful lurch as I backed out and I thought it was the state of the ground. But when Sharon told me about it this morning, I realised it must have been h-his foot... Oh, God!' She collapsed onto the nearest chair.

'So it wasn't deliberate,' said Ted.

'Deliberate? *No!* Of course not! We don't—don't exactly like one another, but I'd never do a thing like that!'

'Are you sure about this, Yona?'

'That I ran over his foot? I must have, mustn't I? He was standing right beside my car, I backed out at speed—and next day he's got a crushed foot.'

'That's certainly how it looks,' he said heavily. 'My God, what a thing to happen! Lucky for you, Mike's not the vindictive type.'

'He's not?' Yona asked doubtfully.

'No, he's not—though it'd take a saint to overlook this and Mike's no more of a saint than the rest of us. I hope you realise what a mess you're in,' he ended.

'Only too well,' sighed Yona.

Ted scratched his chin thoughtfully. 'I have to dash off now to a board meeting and tonight Meg and I are having people in, but I'll talk to Mike tomorrow and—'

'No!' she protested violently. 'I've no intention of hiding behind you. I did it and I'll take the consequences—whatever they are. I'll see him myself.'

Ted eyed her with something like respect. 'You may be a careless driver, but you can face up to things—I have to give you that.' He reverted to the present. 'Are there any problems on the unit before I go?'

'No—none. It was all quiet when I left.'

'Just as well,' said the boss as he went off, shaking his head.

Yona couldn't face the staff canteen for lunch. Mike may or may not already have pointed the finger in her direction but, either way, she'd feel terribly guilty if she heard any talk of his accident. And—horrible thought—he might even be in the canteen himself. By all accounts, he was dedicated enough to be working that day. She bought a sandwich to eat in her room, but first she checked with Ortho to see.

'Sorry, Dr MacFarlane,' she was told, 'but Mr Preston has sustained an injury to his right foot and won't be in before Monday. Would you like to speak to his registrar?'

It was the obvious question, but Yona hadn't foreseen it. She mumbled something about it not being urgent and rang off.

She would have to go and apologise to him at home, then. But first there was the afternoon to get through.

She was down to lecture to physiotherapy students. The talk she gave she'd given several times before in Edinburgh so she was confident and it was well received. But when it came to questions afterwards she soon discovered that—like students north of the border—they were adept at putting queries that were hardly mainstream.

'Please, Dr MacFarlane, why don't animals get rheumatoid arthritis?'

'Why do people not get distemper or hardpad?' asked Yona. 'I think you'd better ask a vet that one—I'm afraid I don't know.'

Next. 'Why aren't copper bangles available on the NHS?'

That was a bit easier. 'Because only remedies which have been proven effective in clinical trials are prescribed. Now, if anybody has a question relevant to my lecture...'

As with students everywhere, that was the signal for a

general exodus and Yona was free to give her mind to the problem of Mike Preston's foot. Back in her room in Outpatients, she was trying to think how in the world she could ever apologise sufficiently when the plaster technician rang to ask if she'd remembered she was deputising for Dr Price today.

That meant two or three hours of making plaster splints for the new ward patients and it was well after six when Yona eventually parked in her place in the underground garage at Park View. The block was L-shaped and, as always, she was glad that Mike lived in the other wing, about as far as possible from her own flat.

The nearer she got to his door, the less confident she felt. This was the most difficult thing she'd ever had to do.

After two rings, and what felt like hours, Mike came to the door himself. He wore a loose, dark sweater which had seen many better days and a pair of scuffed jeans with the right leg chopped off at the knee to accommodate a bulky below-knee plaster, with a weight-bearing rubber rocker under the sole. His foot had been immobilised in slight plantar flexion and an old sock over the forefoot prevented Yona from seeing the damage to his toes, which must have been considerable.

'To what do I owe this pleasure?' he asked after an awkward few moments of charged silence.

Yona raised her anguished eyes from his foot to meet his steady stare and her heart missed a beat from sheer fright. 'I—I thought I ought to come,' she got out at last in a wobbly voice.

Mike looked puzzled. 'Because you're a neighbour, or because it's an old Scots custom?' he asked.

'I'd like to think that the English also apologise for causing serious bodily harm,' she faltered. She was doing this badly. And she'd meant to be so quiet and restrained and dignified. No wonder he was looking as though he didn't know what on earth to make of her!

She must try harder. 'I've not come here to make excuses,' she said more steadily, despite a quivering bottom lip. 'I was careless—criminally careless—and I'm dreadfully ashamed and appalled. I hope you can accept my sincere apologies for running over your foot—but if you can't, I—I really couldn't blame you.'

There! She'd done it. Not very well, but at least it was over...

After what felt like a decade, Mike asked with surprising mildness, 'Is that it, then? No flowers or hot soup for the injured party?'

'I was afraid that if I bought a—a peace-offering, you'd think I was trying to buy you off,' she whispered.

'I'm not easily bought,' said Mike in the same mild way.

'I can believe that,' said Yona. What she couldn't believe was that he wasn't raging and swearing and calling her every kind of maniac, which was what she'd been expecting from a plain-speaking, down-to-earth Lancastrian who had disliked her from the start.

'I don't know what happens in cases of injury inflicted by a motorist on private land,' she ploughed on earnestly. 'I mean, had it been on the highway then the insurance would...would...' His calm, contained manner was proving more unnerving than any amount of rage. 'Tell me what you expect of me and I'll do my best to comply,' Yona wound up awkwardly.

'Will you, now?' he asked thoughtfully. 'Well, suppose you begin by coming in and making me an omelette or something? This foot throbs rather a lot if I stand on it for any length of time.'

'*What?* Yes, well, if that's what—' But he was already

limping away down the corridor so Yona went in and shut the door.

'This is the kitchen,' said Mike, turning round so abruptly that Yona very nearly knocked him down again.

'Er, right! An omelette, you said...'

'Anything you like. I'm not fussy—just hungry. There's plenty of stuff in the fridge. I'll leave you to it, shall I? This is such a small kitchen.' He turned round and limped out.

At least twice the size of mine, she was thinking when he came back to say, 'You'll be making enough for yourself, too, of course—it'll be way past dinnertime when you get home.'

Yona stared up at him, trying desperately to fathom his mood. 'Coals of fire,' she said at last.

A smile flickered at the corner of his mouth for a microsecond before he responded, 'If you like.'

He'd been right when he'd said his fridge was well stocked. Either he was an enthusiastic cook or, more likely, some devoted girlfriend did his shopping. A lot of women still went for the strong, silent type and bachelor doctors had the same attraction for women as honey pots for bees.

Something quick, thought Yona, before he comes round and starts throwing things. She made a *gratinée* of eggs Basque with pasta shells, and chopped a small ogen melon in half to be filled with some thawed-out raspberries for dessert. 'And if he's still hungry after that, he can have some cheese,' she muttered, before calling out, 'Would you like it on a tray or what?'

'In here,' he called back.

She found him in a living room which, like the kitchen, was twice the size of hers. A round, glass-topped table by a picture window was already set for two. A bottle of very good burgundy stood ready on a side table. 'I prefer red,' he said, following her glance.

'So do I,' said Yona.

'But do you think you should?' he asked slyly. 'After all, if you're planning on driving anywhere later on...'

'Please don't remind me,' she pleaded.

'I'm sorry you've forgotten so soon.'

'I have not forgotten—of course I've not. Only with you being so...so *nice* about it...'

'You feel a little less guilty?'

'I suppose so—yes. But I'm still mortified and very sorry!'

'Good—but, there, it wasn't deliberate, was it?'

'Good God, no! Of course it wasn't.

'Ted asked me that,' she said when she'd been to fetch the rest of the food and been told her cooking obviously surpassed her driving skills.

'Asked you what?' asked Mike, through his first mouthful of food.

'If I'd run over your foot deliberately.' Amazing how easy it was to say it now.

'You told *Ted*?' Mike looked and sounded absolutely horrified.

'But of course. I didn't want him to hear about it from anybody else.'

'I can't wait to hear his reaction,' he said half to himself. 'Have you, er, confessed to anybody else?' he asked.

'No—and I suppose that was rather cowardly.'

'Not at all. Rather sensible, I'd say. This egg, cheese, vegetable thing is quite wonderful,' he went on before Yona could ask why it had been sensible. 'If you get struck off for violence towards a superior, you can open a restaurant and make a fortune.'

'Thank you,' said Yona, 'but I'd rather stick to medicine.'

'I'd almost forgotten what a dedicated career-girl you are,' said Mike, sounding disapproving now.

'If that means loving my job and trying my best to be really good at it, then, yes, I suppose I am.'

'Did you know that Meg Burnley was the gold medallist of their year?' he asked with apparent irrelevance.

'No, I didn't,' said Yona, much surprised. 'I knew they'd been students together and I just assumed that Meg wasn't all that bothered about a career—especially as they married so young and started their family almost straight away.'

'Oh, Meg was keen enough on medicine—just a lot keener on Ted,' Mike said firmly. 'Anyway, she's been doing a few sessions per week in a community health centre for some years now.'

As if that was any substitute for a serious career, thought Yona, but she just said neutrally, 'That all sounds very convenient.'

'It's certainly made for harmony in their marriage,' Mike said roundly.

'When the woman makes all the sacrifices, it usually does,' murmured Yona in reply.

He fixed her with a level stare across the remains of their meal. 'That remark was very revealing,' he said slowly. 'I can think of several ways of answering—none of which you would like. So I suggest we have coffee instead.' He got up from the table and began stacking plates on the trolley.

'Here, I'll do that,' she said, getting up and rushing round the table.

'Are you still feeling guilty?' asked Mike.

Yona eyed him sideways under her lashes. 'Why do I

have this feeling that you're making fun of me?' she wondered aloud.

'I wouldn't dare,' he claimed. 'Dedicated career-women like you frighten the life out of me.'

'That's not fair!' she protested, hurt beyond reason.

'The response of the playground,' he returned, unruffled.

'Perhaps there's hope for you after all.' He steered the trolley across the room and lumbered out.

Yona followed him, frowning. She'd give a lot to know what he'd meant by that last remark. What he meant by this whole incredible evening, come to that...

In the kitchen, Mike was filling the kettle. When he opened the dishwasher Yona said, 'Here, I'll do that.'

He stood aside and watched her rinsing plates and cutlery under the cold tap. 'Surely, if they're going in the dishwasher...'

'This only takes a minute or two and it saves having to wash the filter so often,' she explained.

'You're very efficient,' he told her, making it sound more like a criticism than a compliment.

'I'd have thought that was a very good thing in a doctor,' she retorted, stung.

'You're also rather sensitive,' he said.

'For heaven's sake, stop analysing me and tell me where you keep the coffee,' she said irritably as the kettle came to the boil.

'One thing at a time,' he said in a soothing tone calculated to do the opposite. 'You've not finished loading the dishwasher yet. The pans can go in, too,' he said, taking coffee beans from a jar and putting them in a hand grinder fixed to the worktop.

'I thought your foot throbbed when you were standing up,' she reminded him.

'It also throbs when I'm sitting down, so—'

'Back to the living room,' ordered Yona, shooing him out of his own kitchen. In the living room she told him to sit on the couch, where she piled up cushions beside him. 'Now, put your leg up there,' she ordered.

'I can't imagine why I didn't think of this for myself,' he said so meekly that she suspected him of laughing at her again.

'Because, like all doctors, you haven't a clue how to look after yourself,' she suggested.

'You'd make a marvellous nurse, Doctor,' he said, folding his arms behind his head and settling down comfortably.

'That's what you told me on my first day at the Royal.'

'Nursing is a very feminine thing,' he observed, watching for her reaction.

'Then why are so many men taking it up nowadays?' she asked smartly, before going back to the kitchen.

When she returned with the coffee-tray he said, 'Self-defence.'

'What is?'

'Men taking up nursing now that so many women are taking up medicine.'

Putting down the tray on the low table in front of the couch meant that their eyes were more or less level. 'You don't believe in sex equality, do you?' she challenged with a steady look.

'That is not a question which can be answered with a simple yes or no,' he was saying as the outside door slammed, startling them both.

Next moment, a small, pale-skinned young woman burst into the room. She was wearing a neat dark tweed suit and her straight brown hair was held back, childlike, with an Alice band. Her eager expression crumpled with disappointment as she took in the cosy spectacle of Mike lounging on the couch, with Yona kneeling beside him and holding the cafetière, ready to pour out.

Mike didn't help things by reminding the girl, 'You said you were going straight home after your evening class, Fran.'

'After we heard about your foot, Clare offered to sit with Father so that I could come and see you,' she replied, her eyes fixed suspiciously on Yona.

'Dr MacFarlane called round to, er, sympathise, and stayed to cook supper,' Mike said evenly. 'Yona, meet a very old friend of mine, Fran Melling.'

'How do you do?' both girls said together and Fran sent Mike a wounded glance for the way he'd described her.

Potty about him, decided Yona as Fran asked, 'Are you new to the Royal, Dr MacFarlane? Mike's never mentioned you.'

'Fairly new,' said Yona. 'I'm barely halfway through my second month,' she added with a slight feeling of surprise. So much had happened in that time.

'I see. Well, it was very kind of you to cook Mike's supper tonight—I'm very grateful.' Then she turned to Mike. 'Clare will come round and cook for you on the evenings I'm teaching next week.'

'There's no need to involve your sister—or put yourself out, come to that,' said Mike with a touch of impatience. 'Besides, I'll be back at work in a day or two.'

'Oh, but you mustn't, dear—really. You said yourself that these things need time to knit together.'

Fractures, thought Yona, feeling guilty again.

'But perfectly well protected in plaster,' he insisted. 'I'm going to work on Monday.'

'If you can go to work then you can come with me to Lucy's engagement party tomorrow,' said Fran with a sudden show of spirit.

'Perhaps—we'll see,' said Mike, sounding like a man who's been outmanoeuvred.

Yona decided that she'd better leave before she got caught up in the lovers' quarrel that was obviously brewing. 'You're in good hands now, Mike,' she said briskly, 'so I'll be off now.' She looked straight at him and added, 'I really am desperately sorry about all this—and I hope you believe that.'

'Please—think no more about it,' he said firmly.

'Easier said than done,' insisted Yona. 'Goodbye, then,' she said to Fran. 'I can see you know how to look after him.'

'Why is that woman so upset about your foot?' Fran asked suspiciously as Yona shut the living-room door. Yona would have liked to have opened it again to hear Mike's reply, but how would that have looked? As it was, his answer was too muffled to be heard.

Before she headed for her own part of the building, Yona stood in the hallway, thinking hard. There had been something slightly unreal about the whole evening. Getting up the courage to go there in the first place. Mike's unexpected restraint. The meal, the conversation and the feeling that what they were saying didn't quite match the unspoken communication going on below the surface.

She thought again about his reaction to her apology. He'd been generosity itself, leaving her feeling sure that he wouldn't be making any trouble for her. That being so, why wasn't she feeling more relieved? And I wonder how we'd have gone on if Fran hadn't come when she did? Now, there was a question!

CHAPTER FIVE

WHEN Yona pulled back her bedroom curtains next morning, the first thing she noticed was Fran, parking her cycle. She knew it was Fran because the girl was wearing the same suit as the night before and her Alice band was glinting in the early morning sunlight. Yona watched her trot eagerly towards the main door and thought, At least she didn't stay the night.

She was sitting at the kitchen table, eating toast and marmalade and reading the *Scotsman*, when the phone rang. Gil, she supposed, going reluctantly to answer it. But it was Mike, and the sound of his deep voice so close to her ear disturbed her more than she liked. 'I've just been on to the rheumatic unit to ask a favour, but they told me you're off this weekend,' he was saying.

'Yes, I— Yes.'

'Is anything wrong?' he asked carefully.

'No... Why?'

'You sounded odd. As though you'd had some—unwelcome news.'

'Oh, no, nothing like that.' Unless, of course, you counted the realisation that he attracted her more than was good for her.

'You're sure?'

Why was he persisting with this? 'I'm quite sure. There was no mail this morning and I've spoken to nobody since leaving your flat last night.' And then, because he'd already mentioned a favour, she asked, 'Was there something you wanted me to do for you?'

'You're very perceptive,' he told her, sounding much less wary now. 'It occurred to me this morning that this enforced idleness provides me with a good chance to work on a textbook I'm updating. Only I'm completely out of scrap paper, so if you happen to be going anywhere near a stationer's today...'

She owed him and she couldn't forget that, but why her and not his faithful slave Fran? 'Yes, I am going shopping later on this morning, so it'd be no trouble to get you some rough notebooks—or anything else you need.'

'That's very obliging of you, Yona, but I only need the notebooks. Thank you—very much.'

'I don't know what you think you have to thank *me* for,' she returned, overcome anew by his forbearance.

'Call it squaring the account,' he said, without clarifying things much. 'Will I see you later, then?'

'Say twelvish—if that's all right with you.'

'Absolutely. I'm not going anywhere,' he said, making her feel guilty again.

As well as the notebooks, Yona stood on Mike's doormat clutching her own laptop word processor and a bottle of the same kind of wine they'd drunk the night before. The wine had been an impulse buy at the supermarket, but now she was here she felt almost shy about bringing it.

Mike answered the door and accepted her gift with obvious pleasure before she thought to pretend it wasn't for him.

'This is very kind of you—and enough notebooks to write a novel. But what's this?'

'My little laptop—just in case you don't have one at home.'

'I haven't, but won't you be needing it yourself?'

'I've not used it since I came down south, so I just popped into Outpatients for it and—'

'The devil you did!' he exclaimed. 'That is, you shouldn't have bothered. Did you...? Were there many staff about? With it being Saturday...?'

Yona couldn't think why he wanted to know that but she answered, 'Only one or two I knew. Though I did bump into your registrar on the way out.'

That produced another smothered exclamation before he asked, 'Did he have—anything much to say?'

'No, he just asked me if I'd heard about your accident, which I must say I found ironic in the circumstances.'

'And what did you say?' he asked quickly.

'Only that I had—and then we both agreed it was a great pity, which it is.' Yona backed away, saying, 'Well, if there's nothing else...' He obviously wasn't going to ask her in this time.

'Hang on!' he said. 'The least I can do is give you lunch. I mean, you wouldn't want me to get drunk alone, would you? And I might—with nobody to help me drink this.' He held up her present.

Alone, he'd said. So the Fran girl wasn't there... 'I suppose, in the circumstances, it's my duty to keep any eye on you,' said Yona, following him into the flat.

He had a lunch of various cold meats, salad and fruit ready in the kitchen. 'You eat very healthily,' said Yona approvingly when she saw that.

He scratched the side of his nose and grinned at her boyishly. 'If you want the truth, I was trying to impress you,' he admitted, 'though I'll probably go and spoil it all with a large slice of apple pie.'

Made by the devoted Fran, no doubt! 'Apple pie just like Mother used to make,' she observed dryly.

The grin disappeared. 'If my mother ever made an apple

pie, I never saw it,' he said curtly. 'She was always much too busy out and about, making money.'

Yona supposed that meant a dead, absent or unemployed father. 'I'm sorry,' she muttered. 'It sounds as though I spoke out of turn.'

'No—I did,' he said hurriedly. 'And we were getting on so well, too. I'd better open the wine before we fall out again.'

'Let me do it,' she offered at once. 'You told me last night how your foot throbs when you stand on it for too long.'

'It does, too,' he agreed, 'though I'd almost forgotten. I wonder why?' He had the cork out of the bottle by then.

'I'd not be surprised if you were fairly drunk already,' Yona suggested slyly. 'You're certainly most unlike yourself today.' Last night, too...

'So, what am I usually like, then?'

'Very nice to everybody but me. Yet when I really give you cause to hate me suddenly you're nice to me as well. I wonder why?'

He thrust a glass into her hand. 'Drink that and stop asking questions I'm not ready to answer,' he ordered.

Being Yona, she couldn't leave it there. 'Try this for size,' she began. 'You've got a friend who badly wants a particular job, but he loses it to an upstart foreigner—and a woman, what's more. So you're ready to hate the sight of her, even before the poor thing puts in an appearance. What are you laughing at?' she demanded as he sat across the kitchen table, grinning at her—and showing as fine a set of even white teeth as she'd ever seen.

'The idea of you as a "poor thing". Anybody less like a "poor thing" I never saw.'

'Never mind that,' said Yona. 'Am I right?'

'But he wasn't to be drawn. 'First impressions aren't

always the right ones. It's just that I believe it's better to get to know people a bit before making up my mind about them.'

'And have you made up your mind about me yet?'

Mike pulled out a third chair and stuck his foot up on it. 'This foot is giving me hell,' he said soulfully.

Perhaps it was and perhaps it wasn't. Hadn't he already told her there were questions he wasn't prepared to answer? And he couldn't have found a better way of reminding her why she was there. 'Have you got anything you can take for the pain?' she asked, falling into line.

'I'd have to be a lot worse than this before I started guzzling pills—especially after half a bottle of wine.'

'Will I fetch you a cushion, then?' She had to be allowed to do something.

'No, it's easing off now I've got it elevated,' he claimed. 'Being a patient is very instructive,' he added.

'Yes—it must be. Oh, God, I feel really terrible about this!' she burst out remorsefully.

'Please, don't,' he said. 'Besides, it's an ill wind that does no good—or however the saying goes.'

'I'm not sure I know what you mean by that...'

He fixed her with a questing look. 'You wouldn't be here and we'd not be talking like this but for the accident, would we?'

'And that's good, is it?' she asked, feeling a little thrill of excitement.

'Supposing you tell me,' he invited.

'Well, obviously it's better than it was before—but I wish it had come about some other way.'

'There are those who claim that the end justifies the means,' he returned obscurely. 'Shall we have coffee now?'

Yona gave up trying to decide what he'd meant by that and told him that she would make it. 'And you'd better go through and put your foot up on the sofa while I sort this mess.'

'Sort— What exactly are you going to do? I'm not familiar with the Scots vernacular.'

Scots vernacular, indeed! 'To sort is to tidy, or mend or straighten out—to put to rights.'

'Thank you,' said Mike. 'I'd no idea that "sort" was such a useful four-letter word.'

'And a sight less vulgar than some,' Yona called after him as he limped away to do as she'd told him and rest his foot.

He turned round, grinning, to say, 'All that stuff about the dour Scot is just a rumour.'

When Yona joined Mike in his spacious and comfortable living room, he was playing with her little word processor. 'I can't seem to get the hang of this,' he said. 'Is there a handbook to go with it?'

'Yes—in my flat. Would you like me to fetch it?'

'Not now, thanks. To tell you the truth, I don't really feel like working at the moment.'

'Your foot is still sore,' she surmised with another of those little twinges of guilt. She poured the coffee, conscious of his eyes upon her, but when she looked up suddenly his face gave nothing away.

She handed him his coffee. 'You must have been lonely down here at first,' he said as he took it.

'Yes, I was,' she admitted, 'and if it hadn't been for Meg and Ted... But, fortunately, ours is a job that doesn't give us much free time.'

Sounding almost unwilling, he said, 'Tell me something about yourself.'

Didn't he know quite a lot about her already? 'What sort of something?' she asked cagily.

'Let's start with that curious name of yours.'

That was easy enough. 'I was given the old Celtic name of Catriona, but it was too much of a mouthful for my three-year-old brother so he shortened it to Yona—and it stuck.'

'It suits you,' he declared.

'Oh, dear!' exclaimed Yona in mock horror. 'Now you have got me worried! Say it quickly and it sounds terribly like the Gaelic for eagle.'

He lounged back on the couch, his eyes exploring her bright, animated face. 'I wouldn't know about that,' he said. 'I was thinking along the lines of an unusual name for—a rather unusual woman. I don't know how your family—and friends—could bear to part with you.'

This was better—a lot better. 'They couldn't,' she claimed. 'Some of them are still in counselling!'

He smiled, before saying, 'All the same, there can't be anyone up there who, well, who matters very much...or you wouldn't have come.'

Better still. He wants to know if I've got a man in my life, thought Yona, but she reckoned it wouldn't do him any harm to go on wondering a while longer. 'I wouldn't quite go along with that, but my career—'

'Means more to you than any man,' he finished for her, sounding disapproving again.

'You're oversimplifying,' she said, before asking bluntly, 'Do you come from a medical family, Mike?'

He was puzzled. 'No—why?'

'Then you don't know how it feels to live in the shadow of a very successful father—and know everybody's watching and wondering whether you can make it on your own, or whether any advancement is all down to family influence. I simply had to get right away to prove myself,' she said earnestly. 'Can you not see that?'

'Because your career is so important to you.'

Why did he constantly harp on that as though it were a sin? 'Of course my career's important to me, but it's just as important for me to know I got this job because I was the best candidate—and not because I'm my father's daughter. And before you ask me how I know that—Ted told me!'

'I wasn't going to ask,' he said, holding out his cup for a refill.

'Don't deny you thought it, though.'

'Let's say I did wonder—at first.'

'But not now?' she persisted.

'No, not now.'

'So, do you think now that I *am* the right choice for the job?' Somehow it was very important to get him to acknowledge that.

'The board thought so—and that's what counts.'

'You're hedging!' she flared.

'Don't be silly! Haven't I said I no longer believe you got the job because of your father?'

Yes, he had, but he was dodging answering the question after that! 'You still think it should have gone to your friend, don't you?'

'Since you insist on probing the corners of my mind, I'm bound to say he could certainly have done with it.'

'But why this job? I was hearing that he's been offered a similar post in South Wales.'

'So he has—but think of all the trouble and expense and upheaval of moving house with a sickly wife and four small children. Although now, as it's turned out—'

'In other words, family men ought to have priority in the job market—best qualified or not! Well, thank you very much, Mr Neanderthal Preston! We certainly know where we stand now. And to think I thought we were—we really were— Oh, blast!' she sobbed, leaping up and banging out of the flat.

Oh the way downstairs she met Fran, coming up.

Fran flattened herself against the wall on the half-landing to avoid the human missile hurtling towards her. 'You want to be more careful or you could break your neck,' she said as Yona flew past.

Yona scarcely heard and she didn't run out of steam until she'd banged her own door shut behind her.

She'd blown it. She'd lost her temper and blown it—but look at the provocation she'd had! What woman of spirit could have acted otherwise? What was the matter with the man? He was attracted to her—she had sensed that—yet he persisted in parading views he must know she didn't hold with. Was he over-honest, perverse or just plain mad?

All the same, she really wished she hadn't blown her top like that. It would have been much better to stay cool and deal with his archaic views in a light, bantering way. And she probably would have if the wretch didn't attract her so much. Why *was* that? She'd never gone in for the strong, silent type before. Come to think of it, she'd never met a man like Mike before...

Thank heaven she'd already told Ted about the accident. Now he'd never guess there was any other reason for the bad feeling between her and Mike.

But if she stayed in, brooding like this for the rest of the day, she'd go mad. So, what to do? First she dialled Gil's number, then hung up before he could answer. Go home for the rest of the weekend? Only four and a bit hours... No, the M6 was no place for somebody as churned-up as she was.

Yona went out and bought a skirt she didn't need, then went to a cinema, but she had to come out soon after, on finding herself sitting beside a groper. Such was life!

Supper was a sandwich because she couldn't be bothered to cook. After that she took a hefty dose of Mogadon and slept so heavily that she woke late with a head that felt like lead.

Rain was sluicing down the windows. A wet Sunday in Salchester. What depressed person could possibly ask for more? Yona went, yawning, to look for the Sunday papers and found a printed card sticking out of her letter-box. It said simply 'Please open your door.'

She did that and there on the mat and reaching almost to her knees was the largest basket floral arrangement she'd ever received. She stared at it, bemused, for several seconds, before bringing it into the flat.

There was a second card pinned to the basket and her heart speeded up as she recognised the neat, purposeful hand. 'I was way out of order yesterday,' it said. 'Can you forgive me? Please try, Mike.'

Her mood changed on the instant. No longer was he the morose, mixed-up monster he'd been for almost twenty-four hours, but a generous, romantic prince of a man, big enough to admit to being in the wrong. She flew to the phone, then changed her mind and shot into the bathroom instead.

Twenty minutes later, fragrant and casual in a flowing skirt and clinging top of subtle pink which made the most of her auburn hair and remarkable eyes, Yona was standing at Mike's door. She was poised to hurl herself into his arms when the door was opened by Fran. She was wearing a headscarf and a heavy mac and could have been going or coming.

'What do you want?' she asked baldly.

Yona blinked, adjusting. 'I came to see how Mike is getting on.'

'Very well, thank you. I'm seeing to all his needs.'

Was she, indeed? Yona was still concocting a suitable reply when Mike called out, 'Who is it, Fran?'

'That doctor who was here on Friday night,' she called back reluctantly.

'Yona! Well, don't keep her on the doorstep,' he shouted, lumbering down the corridor as fast as his plastered foot would allow.

'He says you can come in.' Fran's version. 'So, do you want me to make coffee, then?' she asked, hoping to delay her departure. 'I've just got time...'

Mike patted her kindly on the shoulder, as though she were a nervous patient or a large dog. 'Not at all, my dear girl. You've done quite enough already this morning—and you know your father likes to get to church in good time.'

'I'm sure he wouldn't mind, the way things are. He thinks the world of you.'

She was obviously so desperate not to leave them alone together that Yona found herself pitying the girl. 'Mike, I've brought the handbook for that word processor I lent you,' she said, by way of explaining her call.

That half reassured Fran, while causing Mike to frown. They stood there, an uneasy trio, until Fran said unhappily, 'Well, perhaps I'd better be off—but I'll come back later.'

'Certainly not,' said Mike firmly. 'As I said, you've done quite enough already. Go and help your father—and enjoy the party. Give my apologies to your friend—I'm sure she'll understand. And thanks again, Fran. You've been marvellous...' He had Yona inside and his door shut before Fran could have reached the stairs.

He leaned against the door and looked at Yona for a long moment, before telling her, 'You look wonderful. Do you always look this good so early on a Sunday morning?'

'Unless I've been working all night,' she said, smiling.

'And, of course, finding such a delightful surprise on my doorstep helped...'

'You got the flowers, then.'

'I did and they're quite lovely. But I can't let you take all the blame for that silly quarrel—'

'Let's forget it for now,' he urged. He took the forgotten booklet out of her hand. 'Thanks for bringing this.'

'Now you can get down to some work,' she said, thinking that she must have read too much into the gift of the flowers.

'Work? Only if I've nothing better to do.'

'Such as?'

'Coffee and chat with...my new friend, for instance?'

'Lovely! But you must let me make it,' she offered eagerly.

This time she did put Fran's cookies on the tray and carried it through to the living room, where Mike was lounging on the couch with his injured foot up.

At first they were wary, but gradually the barriers came down as they talked books and music and sport. They soon found that they both loved skiing and Mike told Yona that he'd only got back from Switzerland the day before she'd started at the Royal.

'I should have guessed that was an Alpine tan...' She dimpled at him. 'I'm going to confess something now. You were so casually dressed that I thought you'd come to mend a window or something. Are you offended?'

'Because you thought I looked like a craftsman? Not at all! Have you never heard it said that orthopaedic surgery is just common sense and carpentry?'

'The man's a wit,' she declared. 'I wonder why I never noticed?'

'And why did it take me so long to realise what a provocative little Scotch witch you are?'

'Scots, if you please. Scotch is what folk drink—if they've any sense, that is.'

'Look at my drinks table,' he suggested.

'I already have. It's got just about everything on it, so you're either very hospitable—or a secret soak!'

'Do I look like a man who's hell-bent on ruining his liver?' he demanded.

Yona eyed him as dispassionately as possible—clear eyes, good skin, firm jaw, lean, hard body. She had to admit, 'No, you look to me like a—a sensible man who takes red wine for his heart and the occasional dram for his sanity.' She was very, very pleased with that.

Mike was also impressed. 'What a golden tongue she has,' he marvelled. 'Well, sometimes, anyway. Are all Scots girls like you?'

'Of course not! I'm unique.'

'I believe that,' he said slowly, and there was that in his eyes which was both exciting and rather scary.

'Oh, look! It's stopped raining and the sun's trying to come out,' she said in a fit of unaccustomed shyness. 'What a pity we can't go for a walk.'

'We could go for a drive, though.'

'But how could you—?'

'I couldn't, but you could.'

'And you'd *trust* me?'

'I'd feel perfectly safe—as long as I was actually in the same car with you…'

'Beast!' She threw a cushion which he fielded and tucked behind his head. 'Have you been to the botanic garden yet?' he asked.

'I didn't know that Salchester had such a thing.'

'Salchester's not all dark, satanic mills, you cheeky bundle! It's got a very fine botanic garden, two splendid art galleries, museums, a repertory theatre and one of the finest symphony orchestras in the country. I'll take you to a concert next week if you're very good.'

How could she ever have thought him tongue-tied? The man was a wonderful talker—*and* he shared most of her leisure interests.

'I'll go and fetch my car before the rain comes on again,' she cried.

'Mine is bigger,' he said practically.

That was true—and it was said that if a man was willing to let you drive his car... 'I've hardly ever driven anything that size,' said Yona, her eyes sparkling.

'Then now's your chance,' he said, tossing her the keys.

'You'll have to navigate,' she reminded him as they set off.

'No problem,' he answered, and there wasn't. He gave her clear directions in plenty of time.

The garden was a real surprise—fifty acres or so in the foothills to the north of the city and not very far from the Burnleys' home. Well-planned woodland surrounded every kind of garden, formal and informal, and not far from the car park was a very good restaurant, which overlooked a small ornamental lake.

After they'd had lunch Yona pointed to a row of wheelchairs by the exit. 'Is that not thoughtful of the authorities? I can take you for a breath of fresh air before the rain comes on again.'

Mike looked absolutely appalled. 'I'm not going in one of those contraptions until I'm seventy,' he growled as he pulled a stout plastic bag out of his pocket and wrapped it securely round his plastered foot.

'Oh, Mike!' she protested. 'Do you think you should?'

'If I can't manage, I'll lean on you,' he said with a saucy grin,' but you can't come here without walking round the lake—and it only takes ten minutes.'

But clouds came scudding up from the west and when they were about halfway round the lake the rain came down in torrents. 'Up here,' said Mike, leaving the main path for a gravel track. He was moving with a speed that surprised her.

He's so game, Yona thought admiringly as she followed. 'You've done this before,' she concluded when they'd gained the shelter of a charming wooden summerhouse.

'Me—and every other Salcestrian. It rains rather a lot in these parts.'

'So I've noticed. And I wish I'd thought to grab a headscarf as well when I went home for my jacket. I must look like a drowned rat.'

'You don't look in the least like a drowned rat,' Mike said slowly, drinking in the sight of her. Her wet hair was now a wonderful dark amber and raindrops glistened on her long, thick lashes. 'You look wonderful. Enchanting...'

When his arms went round her, it seemed the most natural thing in the world, and yet... It's too soon, said reason. You don't really know this man. But the first touch of his mouth on hers was enough to stifle thought and kindle all her fire. They clung to one another like the two drowning people they resembled as the powerful attraction between them finally flared into life.

It was both a relief and a disappointment when the door of the summerhouse was flung open. 'Sorry,' said a newly broken male voice. And then, 'It's no go, Betty.'

'Blast,' responded the unseen Betty. 'Taken, then, is it?'

'There's plenty of room,' Mike said grudgingly.

'Nah—wouldn't want to cramp your style, mate. You got here first,' replied the youth. 'I know another place that'll do us.' Clearly shelter from the rain wasn't their first priority.

'Fancy them two—at their age,' giggled the girl as they scampered off.

'What the hell! Our age indeed,' muttered Mike, glaring after them.

Yona peered round him. 'They don't look more than fifteen,' she decided. 'Ah, well, they'll learn.'

'Learn what?' he asked, smiling down at her.

'That sex has its downside—like every other pleasure in life.' She was in control again now.

So was Mike. 'You don't look like a disillusioned old cynic,' he told her half-jokingly.

'I dare say that's because I'm not one—yet! How long do showers usually last in these parts?'

'Three days is the record.'

'Good grief! I'm not staying in this place for three days. I'm off to fetch your car. The path's wide enough for it as far as the foot of this track.' She was halfway down it by then.

'You'll be stopped at the gate,' Mike shouted after her.

'Trust me to think up a good excuse,' she called back.

The gatekeeper insisted on going with Yona to make sure she was telling the truth about her injured friend—and that she didn't drive over the grass. When they dropped him off, Mike asked her how much she'd tipped the man.

'Not a penny—so now which one of us is the cynic?' she asked, laughing. 'I just told him the facts and he was very sympathetic.'

'Bemused, more likely, if you fixed him with those amazing eyes of yours.'

'If you want to think of me as some sort of siren, feel free. It's better than being thought a road hog!'

'I can honestly say I've never thought of you as a road hog,' Mike said firmly.

'Well, that's something, I suppose,' she said demurely as the heavens opened again.

When she'd parked Mike's car in its accustomed place in the underground car park at the flats, she said pertly, 'I do hope you've enjoyed your little airing.'

'You're sounding like a nurse again,' he said sadly.

'That'll be because that's how I feel about you...'

'I don't know any nurses who kiss their patients quite so beautifully as you do,' he murmured.

'You may have a point there,' she allowed.

'On the other hand, asking me up to your place for a nice cup of tea would be a very nursely thing to do.'

'Why my place and not yours?'

'Because a change of scene is very therapeutic.'

'You've got an answer for everything, have you not?' she challenged.

'Not always,' he admitted. 'But I'm working on it.'

'I'm going to get into some dry clothes,' announced Yona as soon as they reached her flat. 'What about you?'

'I don't think anything of yours would fit me.' He grinned.

'Idiot.' She chuckled appreciatively. 'I was offering to fetch something for you from your own place.'

'No need—I dried off pretty well in the car.'

Yona ran a hand down his thigh. 'Your jeans are still quite damp.'

'Careful! For a heady moment there I thought you were making advances.'

'I have never found it necessary to take the initiative,' Yona told him very firmly.

Mike said he could believe that and if she insisted, he'd go and change his trousers while she made that tea she'd promised him.

Yona wondered if his obvious reluctance had anything

to do with Fran's promise to come back later so she claimed to know better now than to try ordering him about.

'You're getting my measure.' He chuckled. 'Shall I go and put my foot up, then?'

'You're learning, too,' she said.

So she put on the kettle, popped some scones into the oven to warm through and went to change into stretch pants and a sensational clinging sweater. Then she buttered the scones with one hand, while blow-drying her hair with the other. It was fluffed out round her head like a russet cloud when she carried in the teatray.

Mike looked up and stared, transfixed. 'You're amazing,' he said slowly.

She'd have preferred beautiful or wonderful or gorgeous, but amazing would do for now.

'You didn't make these,' he said when he saw the scones.

'No—but I can when I've got the time! Actually, my mother sent them—along with the shortbread and the Dundee cake. She's convinced that the English don't know how to bake and she didn't want me to starve.'

'Poor little exile in a strange land where not all the natives are friendly,' he said softly.

'Got it in one!'

'You were supposed to say, 'I know one native who is *very* friendly,'' Mike reproved gently, as he pulled her down on the couch beside him.

'If you want me to be a yes-woman, you'll have to write me a script,' she warned.

'I want you just the way you are, you fascinating, exotic foreigner,' he murmured, kissing her neck with far-reaching results.

It was the summerhouse in the botanics all over again, but this time there were no teenage lovers to intrude. He was getting to her again with a speed and ease which no other man ever had. It was wonderful and it was scary and Yona had never felt less in control. I shouldn't, but I know I will, she was thinking confusedly when Mike suddenly stiffened and loosened his hold on her with a heavy sigh.

He was regarding her with something like anxiety in his eyes as he admitted, 'It's high time I told you something you're not going to like.' His arms tightened round her again. 'Promise me you'll not be angry.'

'How can I if I don't know what it is?' she asked.

'It's just that I'm so afraid... Today has been so wonderful. Much, much better than I dared to hope when I—'

'The suspense is killing me,' she told him, trying to lighten the moment.

'OK, then, it's like this,' he began, just as there came a thunderous knocking and ringing at the door. They stared at one another in amazement and went to answer it together.

It was Fran standing there, and her eyes were great pools of sorrow and reproach. 'So Angie was right after all,' she breathed. 'You *are* here!'

'As you see,' Mike said tightly. He was rigid with anger. 'Aren't you supposed to be at a party?'

'I came round to tell you that my father is in the Royal. He fell and broke his hip—and he won't let anybody fix it but you!'

Yona recovered first. 'I'll get your jacket, Mike,' she said quietly.

'Yes, I have to go,' he said woodenly as he took it from her.

'I realise that. I'm so sorry about your father's accident,' she told Fran.

'Why?' asked Fran coldly. 'You don't know him.' She turned back to Mike, her eyes anxious and watchful.

'I have to go, Yona,' Mike repeated, 'but I'll phone you later. We haven't finished our conversation.'

Yona had not forgotten that, but as she shut the door she thought, There's no need now. I know what you were going to say. It was obvious that Fran was more to him than just the old friend he'd claimed she was.

CHAPTER SIX

'YOU'RE late, Doctor,' observed Sister Evans gleefully when Yona looked into her office just before nine next morning.

'No, Sister. It's just that most days I'm early. Are there any special problems?'

Either there weren't or Sister was too surprised to say so in the face of Yona's crisp comeback.

Actually, Yona was feeling anything but crisp that morning. Last night Nonie had whisked her off to a lively members-only club, where several unaccustomed vodkas had helped to take her mind off the puzzle of Mike Preston and his old friend Fran, although the din of the disco had also given her a headache.

Mike had promised to phone her later—and he hadn't. So, naturally enough, Yona had been asking herself what was a mere six weeks' acquaintance—no matter how strong their mutual attraction—compared with years of friendship and love? Because there *was* love there—on Fran's side at least. Also, Fran was a doormat, and Yona felt she knew enough of Mike's views by now to know that was really how he liked his women.

In the doctors' room she pulled her mind back on course to ask, 'Any problems, Chris?'

'Not for us,' he said, 'but there was a call from Ortho a few minutes ago. Mr Preston thinks that one of our mutual patients may be about to have a flare-up. So I said that you'd go and check her over when you had time.'

'Mr Preston? But I thought... Is he not off sick?'

'Not according to his houseman. He was in at the crack and did a quickie ward round, before going to Theatre to operate on an old friend of his.'

'But, surely, with a serious injury to his foot...'

'You specialists.' Chris laughed. 'OK, so a ruptured Achilles tendon is no fun, but they mend all right in plaster. Mine did, and I did mine in exactly the same way. I've given it up now, though.'

'Given what up?' asked Yona, now thoroughly confused.

'Squash. It's the worst thing for it, apparently. Didn't you know that?' he asked, noting her dazed expression. 'Fancy me knowing something you don't! That gives me no end of a kick.'

Yona felt as though she'd been kicked, too—right smack in the teeth. What the hell had Mike thought he was doing—letting her take the blame for a sports injury she'd had nothing to do with? And then stringing her along like that, exacting penance the way he had! God, how he must have laughed at her! He'll not be laughing by the time I've finished with him, Yona vowed fiercely. She was desperate to tackle him, but had no chance. Personal problems must be on hold for the next eight hours or so.

'I believe you have a patient for me, Sister,' she was saying to Sister Evans's opposite number on Orthopaedics about ten minutes later.

'Yes, Dr MacFarlane. As you know, Mrs Rathbone had excision of the metatarsal heads, right foot, last week, and now she's complaining of pain in her left knee. Mr Preston has seen her and he's fairly sure it's not a generalised problem but, knowing how keen Professor Burnley is to catch them early...'

'Point me in the right direction, Sister, and I'll give you my opinion—for what it's worth.'

Yona had been speaking as normally as she could because this nice woman had no idea that the visiting doctor would much rather give the wonderful Mr Preston a fist than an opinion!

'The knee is certainly swollen and slightly red, but I can't detect signs of activity in my other joints, Sister,' she said later, 'but an ESR should confirm or exclude that.'

'I thought you'd say that so I've made out a form for you to sign.'

'Bless you and your second sight,' Yona told her gratefully. What a nice change she was from her counterpart on Rheumatology.

'There is a large, noisy crowd of medical students hanging about outside the doctors' room, waiting for you, Dr MacFarlane,' Sister Evans was quick to tell Yona when she got back to base.

'Good,' said Yona, unruffled. 'I hate to be kept waiting.'

'Please, don't let them upset the beds, Doctor.'

'Or the patients either, if I can help it, Sister.'

'And Mr Preston was on the phone while you were absent from the ward.' She made it sound as though Yona had gone AWOL. 'He wishes to see you in his consulting room at your earliest convenience.'

Did he indeed? 'Thank you, Sister. Outside the doctors' room, I think you said...'

Yona slipped into top teaching gear. 'Last week,' she reminded the students, 'you sat in on a clinic and saw how we assess patients who have never been to us before. Today we'll be looking at ward patients. Would anybody care to tell me what sort of problems you can expect to see?'

She may as well have asked them the time of the next bus to the moon for all the response she got. Desperately afraid of saying the wrong thing, she guessed, remembering her own student days.

'Let me put it another way. What do you definitely not expect to see?'

'Multiple fractures,' said somebody at the back. Not quite right when you remembered Mrs Teale and her osteoporosis, but Yona knew what he meant.

'Respiratory failure.' That was the next suggestion.

'Transplant patients.' That was the third.

'We're narrowing it down,' agreed Yona, raising a weak giggle and breaking the ice as she'd intended.

During the next couple of hours she gave them an insight into the routine treatment of the acute phase of rheumatoid arthritis. She also taught them to recognise the radiological differences between the main types of arthritis and then discussed the pros and cons of the various drugs available.

'On Wednesday I shall expect each one of you to take a history from a patient and make a tentative diagnosis,' she warned, 'so spend some time in the library before we meet again.'

When they had gone, Yona glanced at her watch and saw it was almost lunchtime. Good! No time now to answer Mike's summons—and if he followed routine, he'd be taking a clinic at the General Hospital this afternoon.

'How was Windermere?' asked Ted when Yona joined him for their usual Monday sandwich lunch before the week's biggest clinic.

She looked blank.

'Windermere,' he repeated. 'Big stretch of water. Largest lake in England. You were going there yesterday with that sleazy media bloke you've made such a friend of.'

'It just wasn't the day for it.' It sounded better than saying that she'd completely forgotten the arrangement. Another spot of accounting in store, then. 'Poor Gil!' she protested for the look of the thing. 'That's a terrible way to describe him.'

Ted obviously didn't think so, judging by his expression. 'OK, so what did you do instead?' he wanted to know.

'Went for a walk in the afternoon and got thoroughly wet—and then Nonie Burke took me to one of her clubs in the evening.'

'You'd have been better spending the day with us,' Ted said firmly. 'Incidentally, you'll have heard by now, of course.'

'Heard what?' Yona was expecting him to say something about Nonie, but he went on, 'How Mike really got his ankle injury. That must have been a great relief to you.'

'Oh, that... Yes, it was. I'd have hated to be up before the bench on a charge of road rage.'

'Yet you seemed so sure that you were the one who'd done the damage.'

'I was—at the time. A case of putting two and two together and making thirteen. But, then, maths never was my strong point.'

'Is anything wrong, Yona?' Ted asked keenly.

'Not a thing, boss. Why?'

'You seem kind of uptight, that's all.'

'I can't think why,' she maintained.

Ted jumped to the wrong conclusion. 'Don't you let that telly man upset you, my girl,' he advised. 'You can do better than him.'

'If I thought I couldn't, I'd book into the convent right now,' she promised, raising a smile and easing the tension.

It was a very busy afternoon, now that Yona was seeing her own new patients as well as a fair share of the follow-ups. 'I think I'll take the gold,' said the first new one.

For a mad moment Yona thought she was referring to a medal, before she suggested, 'Supposing we start at the beginning, Mrs Trubshaw. I'm Dr MacFarlane, Professor

Burnley's chief assistant. Please sit down and tell me all about it.'

'I've got bad arthritis and I want gold injections. None of those steroids for me, thank you. They only make you fat.'

Whatever she'd got, by observation alone she wasn't too seriously affected so Yona said soothingly, 'With a bit of luck, you'll not need either. We've got lots of other remedies up our sleeves which aren't nearly as drastic. Now, tell me your problems—from the beginning.'

Mrs Trubshaw took Yona at her word. 'Well, now, it all began one evening about four months ago. I'd just put on the kettle for my hot bottle—I don't hold with electric blankets, haven't had one in the house since my dad nearly set himself on fire with one. And then, all of a sudden…'

Yona had never heard anything like it. 'Just like A Book at Bedtime,' she told Ted and Charlie afterwards. 'Anyway, I'll know for sure when I get the lab reports, but I'm nearly sure she has a self-limiting non-specific arthritis of infective origin.' She paused. 'But I'm afraid the next two I saw will have to go on the waiting list. They're both on steroids already and both are going out of control.'

'Steroids are a double-edged sword,' sighed Ted. 'Well, that sounds like an ambulance arriving now, so on with the show, folks.'

Much to Sister Evans's annoyance, Yona had to admit her first follow-up patient. 'But that means I won't have a male bed for an emergency, Doctor!'

'This man is an emergency, Sister. He has chronic lumbar spondylolisthesis and now has marked weakness in both legs, with sensory changes as well.'

'Has the professor sanctioned this?' the sister queried.

'Of course,' answered Yona firmly, knowing that Ted

certainly would, but she took the precaution of telling him before Sister could get at him.

'She'll be questioning my findings next,' he said crossly. 'I hope she doesn't give you a bad time while I'm in Lausanne.'

'Don't worry, Ted—you'll only be away two days. I reckon I can survive that.'

Next came another back—a case of severe and intractable pain. 'My doctor suggested I go to an osteopath,' said the man, 'but they cost money and my mate says there's a girl in Physio here who's magic. So how about it, Doc?'

'Your mate is quite right, by all accounts,' said Yona, hiding a smile. 'Right! Let's see if you're a suitable case for manipulation, shall we?'

After that, it was pairs all the afternoon. The two backs were followed by two pairs of osteoarthritic knees—both with an occupational overlay. First an office cleaner and then a carpet layer. Yona referred all four to Physiotherapy and hoped the department wasn't overlooked already.

Yona was hardly in the flat that night before somebody came hammering on her door. Immediately she thought of Mike, but when she opened up it was to find Gil on the landing.

He was furious. 'I'm not used to being stood up,' he growled without any preamble.

'Yes—about that,' she said. 'I'm very sorry, but something came up. Anyway, we couldn't have gone, could we? Not in all that rain.'

His expression was telling her what he thought of that for an excuse. 'There are such things as contingency plans—which wouldn't have been necessary. The weather was fine in the Lakes.'

'You went anyway, then.'

'Of course—with a girl from casting. She's not as good as you to look at, but she's a lot more straightforward and obliging.' No prizes for guessing what he meant by that.

'Everybody happy, then,' called Yona as he stormed off. She was damned if he was getting the last word.

She'd been all steamed up to give Mike the dressing-down of his life. Now she had to wait. She couldn't settle, though, and prowled about the flat, rehearsing the phrases that would make him see how disgracefully he'd behaved. She had made a mistake that anybody might have made in that situation—and he had taken advantage of it to get her doing his bidding like a slave.

He'd been less than frank about his long-time girlfriend, too. Does he want us both dangling after him? she wondered. Well, you've picked the wrong one here, buster! With me, it's one to one or nothing.

But when he eventually rang her bell and she opened the door to see him standing there, so big and solid and desirable, she forgot all the cutting things she'd planned to say. 'Was there something?' she asked. It was the best she could do, and she only got that out with a lot of effort.

'Of course there is!' he answered roughly, shouldering his way in.

Yona shut the door and leaned against it. She needed some support.

But Mike stomped on to the living room and she had to follow. He had parked himself with his back to the side table where she'd placed his flowers and he said accusingly, 'You've been avoiding me today!'

So it was all her fault, was it? The injustice of it provided some of the stiffening Yona needed. 'I've been very busy today. I've also found out what a fool you've been making of me.' Not bad as far as it went, but hardly the telling-off she'd planned. What's come over me? she wondered.

'You're referring to this.' He slapped his plastered leg. 'What else?'

'I should have put you straight right away—and you must be wondering why I didn't.'

'I know why you didn't! It pleased you to—to humble me and make me dance attendance on you like some eastern slave girl!'

'Not at all. The fact is, I was so fascinated by the transformation from competent, hard-headed modern careerwoman to—to an anxious, sweet, caring, warm and gentle girl that I wanted to keep you that way as long as possible.'

'Well, at least you're honest about it,' she allowed. 'But how very disappointed you must have been when I blew my top about your precious friend David.'

'I blame myself for that. I provoked you.'

It was difficult to go on being mad at a man who came up with such reasonable answers. 'Yes, you did—and I'm not going to deny that. All the same, you should have told me sooner how you injured your foot—yesterday morning, for instance.'

'Would we have had the wonderful day we did if I had?' She had to admit he was right there. 'And I was trying to tell you last night when Fran came hammering on your door.'

'Yes, about your old friend Fran! You've not been quite honest about her, have you?'

'Now why do you think that?'

'Let me put it this way. I've got a few dear old friends of my own—but I wouldn't spoil a date for any one of them because my father had broken his leg.'

'Put it like that, and her behaviour does seem extreme—only that's not how it is. Fran's father is as much my friend as she is. More so, really—I'm under a great obligation to him.'

'I see,' Yona said coolly.

'I doubt it,' he said, sensing her disbelief. 'Dr Melling was my father's best friend and after Dad died he helped me through medical school by every possible means, including a loan. As for Fran...well, she was just always around. And, believe me, that is all!'

Perhaps it was—as far as he was concerned—but it was plain to anybody with eyes in her head that Fran adored him. 'If you say so,' she said, willing to leave it there for now.

'I do—and now we've settled that, how about something to eat? Or have you had supper?'

'No, somehow I've not got round to it...'

'Good. There's a very nice little bistro just across the road so long as you don't mind being seen out with a cripple.'

'What's wrong with the original cover story? If anybody asks, you're my victim and I'm doing penance,' she suggested, turning away to fetch a jacket and missing his look of disappointment.

The bistro was barely half-full. 'It's always the same on Mondays,' Mike told her. 'But at weekends it's necessary to book.'

'Yes, I'd gathered that you're a regular here,' remarked Yona. The patron had greeted Mike by name, before showing them to a corner table well away from the doors and draughts.

'Me—and half the occupants of Park View,' he went on. 'Pierre says he's thinking of renaming the place the Park View Diner. What do you fancy?'

'To eat or as a name for the place?'

'Sharp as a needle,' he said with gratifying admiration.

'A woman in our line of business needs a ready tongue,' she retorted, but she was sorry that they seemed to be off on the same old track before the evening was half an hour old.

'We're not at work now,' he reminded her.

'Neither we are,' she agreed, 'but, work or play, what you see is what you get.' That was her way of telling him she wasn't going to pretend to be anything she wasn't just in order to please him and fit in with his idea of the perfect woman.

'You're utterly honest, aren't you?' he asked. 'I like that.'

They chose the same food—potato and leek soup, with a Normandy peasant dish of lamb and vegetables to follow. 'Leave out the herbs and the butter and the garlic and you've got scouse,' said Mike.

Yona had never heard of scouse, but she supposed that it must be very bland without those additions.

'It is, but generations of Liverpudlians grew up on it. Hence their nickname—Scousers.'

'How come a Salcestrian knows that?'

'My father came from Liverpool and went to school and university there. Then he came to Salchester and met my mother.'

Why does that bitter note creep into his voice whenever he mentions his mother? wondered Yona.

'He was a schoolmaster at an inner city comprehensive,' Mike ended on a note of defiance.

'Then he must have been a good and remarkable man,' she said.

'He was, but how would you know?' he asked keenly.

'Because it's so difficult to teach in such schools.'

'It is, but—'

'How would I know? Because my brother tried it until his health cracked under the strain. He's a Church of Scotland minister now.'

'Why didn't he do medicine?' asked Mike.

'Because he didn't want to,' she answered simply.

'Your father must have been very disappointed.'

'I rather think he was, but, then, he'd always said he'd never pressure either of us into jobs we didn't want or weren't suited to.'

'Then your father is a remarkable man too, Yona.'

'Naturally, I think so.' This exchange of backgrounds was all very well, but Yona hadn't been satisfied by his explanation about Fran. How could she bring the conversation round to her again without seeming too obvious?

'Thanks, but I don't think I could manage a pudding,' she said when the waiter removed their plates and hovered expectantly. 'But don't let that stop you, Mike.'

'It won't,' he said. 'I'm going for cheese, though—and coffee, of course.'

'What would we doctors do without our regular shots of caffeine?' she asked, still wondering how to bring the conversation back to her rival—as she thought of Fran.

'Go to sleep when we ought to be awake,' returned Mike. 'Are you sure you don't want anything else?'

'I wouldn't mind trying a morsel of your Camembert. It looks just right.'

'Anything to oblige the girl I'm trying to impress,' he said, before putting some on a fragment of biscuit for her. Just as he was reaching across to pop it into her mouth, a young couple stopped by their table, looking curious.

'So here you are, Mike,' said the woman, but her eyes were on Yona.

Mike looked up. 'Hello, you two,' he said easily. 'I don't think you've met Yona MacFarlane, have you? Yona—my friends and next-door neighbours, Angie and Simon Bertram.'

'You'll be the doctor Fran was telling us about,' said

Angie flatly as she and her husband sat at their table without being invited.

Yona decided it would be interesting to hear how Mike dealt with that.

'That's right. Yona is the new registrar on Rheumatology at the Royal.' That was how.

'Isn't that the job that was promised to David Lewis?' Angie asked, her cool glance still on Yona. Yona felt she could easily dislike this woman, but again she left it to Mike to explain.

'I don't think there were any promises made, but he certainly hoped to get it,' he said.

'And now they've got to move all that way down to South Wales and poor Sybil so unwell!'

By then Yona had had enough of Angie's tactlessness and she decided it was time to have her say. 'What a pity I didn't know all this before I came,' she said. 'Then *I* could have applied for the Cardiff job instead—and everybody would have been happy. After all, it made no difference to me where I went—as long as I got promotion.'

'Quite,' agreed Angie, while Simon buried his red face in the menu and Mike looked distinctly put out.

'You know Gil Salvesen, don't you?' Angie's next barb.

'We live on the same landing,' returned Yona, determined not to show her irritation. 'One generally does know one's neighbours, don't you find? Whether one wishes to or not.'

Simon gave Yona a glance of respect for that and Mike smothered a smile. 'We're way ahead of you two,' he said, 'so I'm sure you'll excuse us if we leave you to it. Incidentally, the lamb is particularly good tonight.'

He got to his feet, helped Yona into her jacket and they all said goodnight. Yona could feel at least one pair of hostile eyes boring into her back as they crossed the room.

'Don't mind Angie,' said Mike as they returned to the flats. 'She and Fran and Sybil Lewis are great pals, having been at school and university together. They were known as the three Graces then.'

'No wonder Angie was so hostile to me. On Fran's account, as much as on the Lewises',' she persisted when he didn't comment. 'I suppose you realise that the first thing she'll do when she gets home is to ring up Fran and tell her who you were with in that bistro tonight?'

'Yes, of course I do!'

'And you don't mind?'

'Why should I?' he asked a shade impatiently. 'I've already made my position quite clear to Fran.' But after a tiny pause he added, 'All the same, it might be better if we don't go there again.'

'To the bistro?' He nodded. 'Because Fran is so sensitive?'

'You've got it,' he said gratefully.

Oh, yes—she'd got it, and it was just as she'd thought. Fran might be on the back burner while he indulged his fancy for herself, but she was still there in the background, with feelings that mustn't be hurt.

'No, don't bother to come up with me,' said Yona, when Mike had walked her to the main door of her wing. 'Fran doesn't have an exclusive on sensitivity and Angie managed to upset me back there. Now I'm feeling hurt and also rather guilty, which is simply not fair. But thanks for dinner, Mike,' she went on, cutting across his protest. 'That was really kind of you. You must let me return the compliment some time.' Then she let herself in and left him staring after her through the thick plate-glass door.

She scorned the lift and took the stairs and when she turned the corner on the top floor Mike was waiting outside her door. She stared at him, amazed. 'How did you manage that?' she asked.

'The same key opens both main doors and I took the lift.' He paused, eyeing her sombrely. 'Wouldn't a better question be—why?'

'All right, then. Why?'

'Because I was damned if I was going to let you go like that—just because of something that wretched woman said. She's too prejudiced to take a balanced view about—anything.'

People were coming down the corridor so she said, 'You'd better come in.' But she was thinking that if Angie was prejudiced in favour of her friends, then so was he—at least until very recently.

In the living room, she tossed her jacket onto the nearest chair and went over to the drinks cupboard. 'Can I get you something?'

'Nothing, thanks.' He came right up behind her and said quietly, humbly, 'Yesterday I was happier than I've ever been in all my life. Now, tell me what you make of that.'

The current of emotion that charged through her at his words made it impossible for Yona to say anything at first. Then slowly, cautiously, she said, 'I was—fairly happy too. Until Fran came.'

'I had to go,' he said, pleading for her understanding. 'Doc Melling has been like a second father to me.'

Yona turned round to face him. 'I understand that. It's your relationship with his daughter I'm not clear about.'

'But I told you—'

'I know what you told me, but the girl adores you—surely you know that.'

'Of course I know it—but I swear to you, Yona, that I've never done anything to encourage her. I'm fond of her—like I would be of a sister, I suppose. She's a nice, kind, decent girl, but—' He broke off and began to pace about, a nice, kind, decent man with a problem he didn't know how to solve.

'Can you imagine what it's like?' he burst out. 'Owing her father, who knows her feelings as well as I do? And most of our friends, married long since, all hinting and nudging... Never having met my one and only, I'd just about got the length of wondering whether it could possibly work—Fran and me.' He paused long enough to make Yona want to scream. 'Then you came along and blew everything apart!'

'I'd no idea I was so explosive,' she said unsteadily.

'You're the most exciting, most desirable woman I've ever met,' he said in a voice that was vibrant with emotion. He seized her elbows in a grip that hurt.

'You're not the only one with problems,' she faltered. 'I was—dumped just before I came here...'

'He must be insane,' he said, 'but I'm very glad of it!'

Just as before, when he kissed her Yona felt herself responding with a speed and eagerness that blocked out all else.

And, as yesterday, it was Mike who called a halt. 'I'm rushing you...'

'Mmm,' she agreed.

'I'm on call.' Yona hadn't realised that. 'And there's a patient I promised to go in and take another look at...' He kissed her once more, hungrily, unwilling to leave her.

'I understand,' she murmured.

'Yes, you do, don't you? I can sense it.'

'I'm a doctor too, remember.'

'And that has to be a plus at a time like this.' He folded his arms behind her waist and let his eyes roam over her face. 'I'm off tomorrow night, though.'

Yona wrinkled her nose. 'But I'm not. How's that for a plus?'

'Wednesday, then.'

'But will you not be on again?'

'Let me worry about that. There are advantages to being a consultant—even a junior one.'

'Here's to the day when I can say that,' she said, afraid before she'd finished that she'd put her foot in it again.

If she had, he didn't react this time. 'Wednesday, then,' he repeated, 'but I'll see you before that, my wonderful, lovely one.'

He was still gazing into her eyes, and she said reluctantly, 'You mentioned a patient goodness knows how long ago…'

'It's all your fault for being so entrancing,' he whispered. 'OK, I'm really going now. Take care, my dearest girl.'

What harm can I possibly come to in my own home? Yona wondered dreamily as she watched him limp towards the lift. All the same, it felt rather wonderful to be worried about and fussed over. If only it wasn't such an age until Wednesday.

CHAPTER SEVEN

THE last time Yona had been on night duty, the calls had come in thick and fast. Tonight, she managed a leisurely supper and was watching television in the residents' quarters when she was called to Orthopaedics to see a male patient who was complaining of chest pain. She swung her legs off the sofa, slipped on her shoes and her white coat and hared off to investigate.

'Operated on early yesterday morning for a fractured neck of femur,' explained the nurse in charge, while hurrying Yona down the corridor. 'The houseman's given him some streptokinase and he's feeling a bit better but, with him being a doctor, we thought we should get you to check him over—just to be on the safe side.'

With information like that, Yona had guessed who her patient was before she saw the name on the door of the side ward. Routine examination convinced her that Fran's father had sustained a mild to moderate myocardial infarct. His grey pallor, shallow breathing and pulse told the tale before her stethoscope confirmed it.

'I'm afraid I'm being rather a nuisance,' said Dr Melling when the examination was over.

Yona smiled at him. 'If you must have an MI, then what better place than a hospital?' she asked. 'Have you ever had anything like this before?'

He read her name badge and his expression sharpened. 'Nothing so severe, Dr MacFarlane. Just the odd twinge which could have been indigestion but probably wasn't— with hindsight.'

'Well, that's the main question asked,' she returned soothingly. 'The others can wait until you've rested.'

'I'm afraid you're going to have to special him,' she told the nurse as they left the room. To the houseman she said, 'You did all the right things, but he'll have to be monitored here. The coronary care unit is already full. Call me at once if there's any change. Otherwise, I'll come back in a couple of hours—just to check.'

So that's the man to whom Mike owes so much, thought Yona as she left the unit. And I could tell he's heard of me. Did Fran tell him where she found Mike on Sunday night, then?

'He's sleeping,' they told Yona when she returned to Ortho in the early hours.

'Then I'll not disturb him, but I would like to see the wave pattern.'

It was exactly what she expected and the patient lay, his eyes closed, relaxed and peaceful. His colour was much better and his breathing easy. As Yona tiptoed away he said, 'I'm not asleep, Dr MacFarlane.'

'Then I'm sorry if I woke you,' she apologised.

'Not at all. I'm a very light sleeper and that door squeaks.' He eyed her in the same keen way as before as he said, 'I think you know my daughter, Doctor.'

'We've met—briefly,' she agreed carefully.

'When she was visiting her fiancé—yes, I'd heard. You and Mike Preston are neighbours, I understand.'

It was cleverly done, the devoted father protecting his daughter's interests. But Mike had interests, too—and so had she.

'Yes, we're neighbours,' she agreed. 'And colleagues, too. I didn't know that he was engaged, though. I must congratulate him next time I see him.'

The old man was taken aback, as she'd meant him to be.

'It's still unofficial so that could be premature, Doctor. I suppose I shouldn't have let the cat out of the bag, but I'm so pleased at the way things are turning out. Mike has been like a son to me since his father died.'

'No wonder he was so distressed when he heard about your accident. You're really in the wars just now, are you not?' Yona asked brightly, doctor to patient. 'I expect Mike will be asking a cardiologist to look you over tomorrow— or should I say later on today? So I'll leave you to rest now. I only came back to make sure you were stable.'

She wrote her observations in his notes and left the room with a final smiling glance. Apparently the perfect professional, but Yona was very uneasy inside. Mike was in far deeper than he realised, or cared to be.

The clinic overran on Wednesday morning and Yona had her medical students coming again at two. She was resigned to another day going by without seeing Mike, but he came into her consulting room just as the last patient was leaving. He looked very serious. 'You're worrying about your friend Dr Melling,' she guessed.

'Yes—it's a pity about the coronary on top of his accident, but the cardiologist isn't unduly concerned.' He frowned. 'Doc Melling told me it was you who was called to him last night.'

'That's right, being duty medical registrar...' She jerked her head in the direction of the clerk who had come to collect the records and X-rays.

Mike fumed impatiently until she had gone and then he said, 'It seems that Fran had told him about you.'

'She certainly had. He told me that his daughter had met me—while she was visiting her fiancé.'

Mike looked poleaxed. 'My God! Did he really say that?

What on earth possessed him? Don't tell me you believed it?'

'Of course not, though I must admit I was...rather surprised.' What an understatement!

'I said I hadn't known about the engagement and would congratulate you next time we met.'

The anguish in his eyes turned to admiration. 'Trust you to come up with the right thing. What did he say to that?'

'That congratulations would be premature as the engagement was still unofficial.' She laid a light hand on his arm. 'All the same...'

'I know! I've let things drift for far too long—hoping that Fran would get the message without me having to spell it out. But, don't worry, I've done it now. She knows exactly where we stand now—though she's obviously not told her father yet.'

'Perhaps she's saving all bad news until he's over this bad patch,' said Yona, hoping she was right.

'Yes, of course—that'll be it. And now isn't it time we talked about something other than the Mellings?'

'Such as?' she asked, smiling up at him.

'Such as what we're going to do tonight.'

'Just don't suggest anything too energetic,' she begged. 'Last night began quietly enough but ended in a deluge so I didn't get much sleep.'

'Poor little girl!' He stroked her cheek lightly with the backs of his fingers. 'I'm on call tonight, but a lot less likely to be run off my feet than you were. So, how about I cook dinner and we save a night on the town for tomorrow?'

'Sounds all right to me,' she said, 'only I thought you couldn't cook in your present disabled state.'

His glance was roguish. 'Only when it suits my purpose—like it did last Friday. So half-six at my place, then—and don't be late.' He dropped a kiss on the end of her nose and let her go abruptly when somebody tapped on the door.

The students trooped onto the unit, looking at once self-conscious and self-important with their new stethoscopes draped round their necks or coiled inexpertly in the pockets of their white jackets.

Yona had secured the co-operation of a dozen willing patients because, as Mrs Kavanagh said, everybody has to learn their trade—even doctors. She handed out the name cards, one per student. 'Take a full medical history and don't forget to ask about the health of their closest relatives. Then carry out the examination. Be gentle—and don't forget to thank your patients for their help. They're all volunteers, you know.'

'Will you be watching us, Dr MacFarlane?' asked one.

'I'll be in the ward, so don't be surprised if I pop my head round the curtains from time to time. And don't be too proud to ask for help—there's no shame in it. I'm forever picking the professor's brains.'

'It's that Sister Evans we have to watch out for,' muttered another.

'Sister Evans is one of this hospital's finest, but she happens to be off duty today,' said Yona, who had made sure of that, before arranging their first practical class.

'I'd have been more than willing to help with the students,' said Mrs Baker reproachfully as Yona passed the end of her bed.

'I know and I'm very grateful,' returned Yona, 'but we only ask patients who are nearly ready to go home—and you're not quite at that stage yet.'

'They set a student on me when I was in Surgical, getting my gall bladder out,' confided the patient in the next bed. 'Poked and prodded something awful, I can tell you. That's not the way to do it, I told him. It'll only come out if you take a knife to it—and Mr Smith'll be doing that.'

Giggles were coming from behind the curtains nearby and Mrs Kavanagh was heard to explain, 'I'm ever so ticklish, but it's all right, love. It doesn't hurt a bit now so you can grab it a bit firmer if you like.' At least one student had taken the 'be gentle' warning to heart!

'Excuse me, Dr MacFarlane, but Mr Jennings says that his grandfather had osteoarthritis. Does that mean that his is hereditary?'

And the prescribed reading of another one had been less than comprehensive! 'There could be some element of it—if your patient has got OA. Has he?'

'I, um, haven't made up my mind yet.'

'Then why not complete your examination? That might help you to decide.'

'I have—and taken his history.'

In ten minutes? That must be a world record! 'You've been very quick, so it's possible that you've missed something. Let me see your notes.'

They were passed over very reluctantly, with a plea for rotten writing to be taken into consideration.

Rotten it certainly was and there wasn't much of it either. 'What happened to the guidelines for examination that I gave you on Monday?' Yona asked patiently.

'I forgot to bring it.'

Yona handed him another, wishing she'd had a hefty bet on that reply. Ah, well, there was usually one in every group...

The examinations completed, they all crowded into the doctors' room for assessment and discussion of their efforts. Yona kept their results—they would provide the basis for her next lecture when she'd fill in the gaps. After that she'd be passing them on to Ted and she wanted them to be well prepared.

No sooner had the medical students gone than a young student nurse was asking, 'Would you come and look at Mrs Finney's arm, please, Doctor? I don't like the look of it.'

Mrs Finney was having a blood transfusion and Yona prayed that the needle hadn't slipped. If blood was leaking into the tissues... That arm was fine, but the other one was bruised from wrist to elbow. 'What on earth—?' began Yona.

'I was reaching into my locker for a book, Doctor, only the door sort of swung to and my arm got trapped. And the more I pulled—well, it was like it had a spring on it. The door, that is.'

'Have you not been warned to be careful when you're so prone to bruises?' asked Yona worriedly.

'Oh, yes—and I am as a rule, only the nurses were so busy and I didn't want to bother them. Have I broken anything?'

'Just the skin in one or two places, but that's bad enough—it's paper-thin.'

'I know! Isn't it amazing?'

Does she think I've paid her a compliment? wondered Yona as she told the nurse how to repair the damage.

'And I think I'll pad that locker door when I've done her dressing,' he muttered. 'I wouldn't put it past her to try that again next time she thinks we're too busy.'

Another good nurse in the making, thought Yona as she went to deal with a crisis in the men's ward. Charlie was off on study leave again.

Mike had said half six, but it was later than that when Yona rang his doorbell. He came to let her in and greeted her with flattering warmth.

'You should have shut the door first.' She laughed. 'Supposing your friendly next-door neighbour Angie had been on the lookout?'

'I shall hug whom I please on my own doorstep,' he said truculently, which wasn't as good as telling her he didn't care who saw him hugging *her*! Still, progress was progress. 'You've still got your plaster boot, I see. Were you not hoping to persuade one of your colleagues to suture the tendon instead?'

'He refused point blank; told me I ought to know I'd get a better result with conservative treatment. Still, there is the plus side. My patients have stopped grumbling at me now I'm one of them.'

'Perhaps we should all take to plaster boots, then,' suggested Yona.

'Perhaps not. Think of the taxi fares for a start. I'll be flat broke by the time I do get the wretched thing off.' He bent down to kiss her again. 'Come through to the kitchen and have a drink or two while I finish off.'

'But you're on call,' she reminded him.

'I know, but you're not—and I'm going to get you so sozzled that you'll not be able to resist my advances.'

She couldn't anyway, but maybe it was as well he didn't realise it! This thing wasn't a week old yet. 'That's real cave-man talk,' said Yona. 'It's a very good thing I don't wear my hair any longer or you might start dragging me about. What are you cooking? It smells wonderful.'

'So it should with half a bottle of my best Beaujolais in it!'

'I hope you'll manage to lift your mind above alcohol some time tonight!'

He ran a hand caressingly down her spine and Yona was

glad she was wearing a sweater over her thin blouse. 'I will, sweetie—don't you doubt it. Above, or maybe below—according to where it comes on your scale of life's other pleasures.'

He was showing her a new side tonight and she wondered where he'd learned his patter. It was brilliant. 'Right now, food is highest up the scale for one who only had a banana for her lunch,' warned Yona, as she lifted lids on saucepans. 'Oh, goodie! I adore pasta. It fills me up and makes me want to go to sleep like a contented cat.'

'That was not the idea at all.' He frowned comically. 'And I'm not having it.'

'So how do you propose to keep me awake, then?' she asked, which maybe wasn't the wisest thing.

'If all else fails, I could always play my trumpet at you,' he threatened.

'You don't! Do you? Play the trumpet...'

'Sadly not now—no time. But I made the National Youth Orchestra, I'd have you know.'

'But surely there's a good amateur orchestra in a place this size,' said Yona.

'There are several, but I could never guarantee to make all the rehearsals. How the hell did we get onto this?'

'You were telling me how you planned to keep me awake tonight.'

'Only as a last resort,' he said with meaning.

'You're on call,' she reminded him.

'Trust you to finger the flaw in my plan! But tomorrow we'll both be off,' he reminded her with another meaningful look.

He refused her help, so Yona watched him piling the food onto plates and enjoyed the look of him—broad-shouldered, neat-hipped, smooth deft movements of capable hands, the fact that he needed a haircut. Even the awkward lurch as he turned round from the stove was endearing.

She relived the horror when she'd thought she'd been responsible for his injury, and was glad. But for that misunderstanding, they could still be fencing warily. Circling, waiting...

'Here, let me take that,' she offered when the trolley was loaded. 'Or, better still, why do we not eat here? There's plenty of room.'

'God, but you're bossy,' he said in a tone that belied his words. 'I don't know how Ted puts up with you. Just bring the other bottle of wine, there's a good girl.' Then he trundled off down the corridor, leaving Yona to follow.

'I was only trying to save you some trouble,' she called plaintively.

'I know—and I appreciate it,' he called back. 'Tell you what, next time I come to your place, you can drop grapes into my mouth while I recline on your couch like an ancient Roman.'

'I'll do no such thing,' declared Yona. 'Eating lying down is just asking for a choking fit.'

'Must you be so literal?' he asked when they were in his spacious living room. 'That was just my way of telling you that next time we dine in you can wait on me.'

'Fair enough,' she said, and then she caught sight of the table with its wonderful centrepiece of flowers and candles. 'Oh, Mike—how lovely! You've gone to so much trouble. Is it your birthday or something?'

'Sort of,' he said obscurely. 'But don't you be thinking I go in for anything so pansyish as flower-arranging. They have these things all ready made up at the florist's opposite the hospital.'

'If only I'd known today was so special, I'd have brought you a present.'

'You have,' he said as they took their places at the table. 'You're here, aren't you? That's enough.'

And his words were enough to make her heart turn a somersault. She could only gaze at him wordlessly in reply.

'You're a very good cook,' she told him when she'd got herself together. 'Most of the men I know live out of packets—or eat out.'

'So did I—once. And then... Have some more wine,' he said quickly, reaching across the table to top up her glass.

Had that been another near reference to an early life he'd already hinted at as being less than perfect? But before she could probe he was saying, 'You're a pretty good cook yourself. That marvellous supper at your house-warming—and last Friday, here.'

'Last Friday,' she echoed, ignoring the first bit because she hadn't cooked that meal. 'Five days. Is it really only that long since—?'

'It's said that sometimes a minute—even a second—is enough. Only I never believed it until now,' he said, holding her gaze across the flowers and the candles.

Again she had that feeling of something that could take her to the end of the rainbow—or else something that could send her life spiralling out of control. There had been too many times before when all had seemed set fair, only to crash messily and painfully weeks or months later. Hadn't one reason for coming to Salchester been escape from the most recent disaster?

'I've never believed it either,' she admitted.

'Well, of course not,' he agreed. 'If we'd already found the crock of gold we'd not be here together like this now, would we?'

That was so obvious as to need no endorsement. 'Let's move over to the fire,' Mike suggested softly.

'All right...' Yona got up too, and bent to blow out the

candles. 'It seems a shame, but they would soon have set light to the flowers if we'd left them.'

'How practical you are,' he said. Had that been praise or disapproval?

'I can't help it—that's the way I am.'

'You never pretend, do you? I like that.'

'Neither do you. It was one of the first things I noticed about you.' That was nearly true, but there had been times when he'd left her puzzled. About his initial apparent dislike of her, about Fran, about his mother...

She wasn't puzzled when he kissed her, though. There was no mistaking the desire, the hunger, in that kiss. Whatever else there was or wasn't between them, there was a deep and demanding attraction that sooner or later had to be satisfied. 'You're on call, Mike...'

'I haven't forgotten.'

'All the same...' The speed with which he could arouse her was wonderful as well as amazing. Yona had never known anything like it. For her, at any rate, the emergency call came in the nick of time.

It was silly, but she was hurt at the apparent ease with which Mike could switch off and reach for the phone, to listen and say matter-of-factly, 'Yes, you were quite right to call me. Tell Theatre to stand by and I'll be there as soon as I can get a taxi. You've sent one? Good girl. I'm on my way, then.'

'It sounds serious,' he told Yona sombrely. 'I could be hours so you'd better go home to bed, my pet. It's fairly late already.'

'I'll tidy up first.'

'No, leave it, dearest. You must be worn out after your own hectic night on. I'll pick you up tomorrow night at seven. The concert starts at half past so we'll eat after it.' He was totally in control and practical now.

'I'll look forward to it,' she said as he scrambled awkwardly to his feet when the entry phone rang.

He pulled her up beside him, kissed her just once—almost briskly—and limped off.

Mechanically Yona cleared the table and dealt with the dishes and pots. Then she also left. As the lift doors swished shut, she heard Fran Melling saying goodnight to her great friend Angie who lived so inconveniently next door to Mike. Would they ever get out from under that girl's shadow?

CHAPTER EIGHT

'IF I were a betting man, I'd start a book on where they'll be putting us next,' grumbled Ted on Thursday morning, when all the doctors had been directed to park on a derelict site behind the boiler house. 'This sort of thing never happened in my great-grandfather's day.'

'Surely the doctors came by horse and carriage in his day,' said Yona, laughing. 'Never mind! The car-park resurfacing will be completed by the end of this week—or so they say.'

'If they'd managed it a bit sooner, you'd not have had your fright,' Ted pointed out.

'What fright?' she asked a second before realising what he'd meant.

Ted was very surprised but, then, he didn't know how miraculously that had turned out. 'Why, thinking that you crippled poor old Mike for life, of course. I wonder what he'd say if he knew?'

'He does know. I apologised as I said I would—and he was...rather amused.'

'Only rather? I'd have expected him to laugh his head off. But he must be very worried.'

'What about?' asked Yona.

'The accident to his prospective father-in-law. Haven't you heard? The poor old chap's in Ortho with a fractured neck of femur.'

Yona wanted to say, Certainly I know—Mike was with me in my flat when he got the news. But how could she? After the way Ted had described Fran's father?

'I was called to Dr Melling on Tuesday night—for a mild coronary,' she said instead. And before Ted could say anything else depressing she said quickly, 'But I want to know all about Lausanne. I'm sure they liked your paper.'

Ted told her she was a flatterer and gave her all the details as they climbed the stair to Rheumatology, but Yona wasn't concentrating. Had Ted been assuming too much—as Fran and her father had—or was Mike being less than honest with her?

She tried to remember exactly what he'd said each time they'd talked about Fran, but Ted was asking too many questions now. Naturally, he wanted to know everything that had happened during his two days' absence. A tall order that, but fortunately Yona had kept notes.

She'd barely got started on her recital, though, when Sister Evans met them on the landing. 'Good morning, Professor—about the medical students,' she began ominously.

'Yes, I gather that's all going very smoothly,' he pre-empted her, conjuring a neat packet from the pocket of his white coat. 'Just a small memento, Sister. I remember how much you enjoyed your holiday in Switzerland a few years back.'

'The only holiday I ever heard of her taking,' he whispered to Yona as Sister—now speechless and pink with pleasure—led the way to the wards, her grievance forgotten.

He always says and does the right thing and never forgets the smallest detail, thought Yona. Which only made his reference to Fran's father more significant.

Ted went straight into action in the women's ward. 'Have the neurosurgeons seen Mrs Baker yet, Dr MacFarlane?'

'Yes, Professor—on Tuesday. And they agree with us

about the need for a permanent collar,' stressed Yona for the patient's benefit. Mrs Baker was against the idea because she'd not be able to wear her pearls.

Ted dealt with her objections kindly but firmly, and they moved on to their newest patient. 'What have we here?' he asked in a low voice.

'Would you believe another SLE?' Yona asked softly.

'Yes, I would,' he answered. 'It's commoner than people think. Remind me to stress that next time we talk to GPs. Right, then!' He held out his hand for the notes.

While he was reading, Yona chanced to glance out of the window. She went rigid with apprehension. Mike was standing by the main door of the surgical block and he was talking to Fran. Why was she here so early when visiting began at three? Had her father had a relapse? As she watched, Fran moved closer to Mike and laid a hand on his arm. He didn't shake it off. Now he was patting her shoulders. No, he wasn't—he'd put an arm round them! Spelt it out to her, had he? Not from where Yona was standing!

Ted had finished reading and he asked Yona a question. When she didn't answer or even seem to hear, he looked out as well to see what she was finding so absorbing. Glancing at her set face, his eyes narrowed thoughtfully.

'I've really nothing to add to Dr MacFarlane's findings,' he told the new patient in a voice loud enough to bring Yona out of her daze. Then he outlined the treatment, told her how fortunate it was that they'd caught her problem so early and that she'd soon be feeling more like her old self.

As expected, Mrs Kavanagh and Mrs Jacobson were considered ready to go home. They had become fast friends during their stay and were, they said, leaving with mixed feelings.

Sister assumed that was because she'd made them so

happy and comfortable, but they weren't letting her get away with that. 'We live at opposite ends of the city, neither of us can drive and buses are impossible,' said Mrs Kavanagh.

'We'd like to meet occasionally, but how can we?' wondered Mrs Jacobson.

In a flash, Ted was away on one of his favourite hobby-horses. 'We can build space rockets, but we can't build buses which don't require the speed and agility of an Olympic athlete! And it's not just the elderly and disabled who have problems. Have you ever seen a short girl in a tight skirt trying to get on a bus with a baby or an armful of parcels?' The patients loved it and when he ran out of steam they gave him a round of applause.

After the round Yona's boss congratulated her on keeping things going so well during his absence.

'I did my best,' she returned, flushing with pleasure at his praise.

'And you certainly succeeded.' He hesitated, before proceeding carefully. 'There's talk of appointing a junior consultant in Rheumatology to be based at the General—probably in the next year or so.'

'Ah,' said Yona, unsure whether or not she was being invited to apply.

From that, Ted assumed that she wasn't interested. 'More or less what I expected,' he said. 'Nobody could blame you if you headed back to bonny Scotland after a decent interval down here. And when I say bonny, that's what I mean. Such a beautiful country!'

Yona couldn't decide what she was being told now, but one point certainly needed to be clarified. 'Is there anything wrong with my work?' she asked bluntly.

Ted looked stunned. 'Good Lord, no! You really must

be wool-gathering to ask that so soon after being praised. We're all delighted with you. I thought you knew that.'

'Thank you. I just wanted to be sure...'

'Well, you can be. I only meant that you'll probably want to return home some time for personal reasons. Family, friends...' His voice tailed off.

'In the long run, who knows?' allowed Yona. 'But for the moment, I'm very glad to be here, enlarging my experience.'

They both refused coffee in Sister's office, pleading pressure of work. Yona was glad to get a few moments to herself. She knew now what Ted had been trying to say. He must have guessed that she was attracted to Mike and wanted to provide her with a good excuse to exit gracefully from the Royal, as and when necessary. She thought again of what she'd seen through the ward window and caught a quivering lip between her teeth. She didn't doubt the strength of the physical attraction Mike felt for her, but was it enough?

What was it the old song said? 'Too hot not to cool down.' Was this just one of those things then? It was beginning to look that way...

This was Yona's day for a clinic at the Salchester General Hospital and what a marathon it turned out to be. No wonder a new consultant post was being considered, especially as more and more general medical beds here were being taken up by rheumatic patients.

By the time she had done a mini-ward round as well, it was way past six and she was faced with a five-mile drive home through crowded streets. Fortunately she had laid out her good green suit and its accessories before she'd left that morning, but she must—simply must have a shower.

Mike was prompt to the minute and Yona was just finishing her make-up when he rang the bell. She took her time about answering. How much mileage was there in this thing when such an authority as Ted Burnley believed that Mike and Fran were an item?

Mike picked up those uncertain vibes as he kissed her, but blamed them on the hectic day she'd almost certainly had.

'No worse than usual,' she told him. 'Rather better, in fact, with Ted back.'

'But something has upset you,' he persisted. 'Have you had bad news from home?'

'Why on earth should you think that?'

'Because if everything is all right at work what else is there?'

She found she couldn't voice her doubts—not while he was looking at her with such obvious warmth and concern. 'Just a wee bit of a headache,' she offered instead.

Mike frowned anxiously. 'Do you often get headaches? Because, if so, you should take advice. Is it bad? Would you rather not go out?'

Yona made an effort. 'To start at the beginning, the answers are hardly ever, it's only a niggle and we are definitely going out.' What had prompted her to make such a wimpish excuse? 'I wouldn't miss this for the world.'

Mike was amused at her vehemence. 'But it's only a routine concert—nothing special.'

'It is so, then—it's my first chance to hear the world-famous Salchester Symphony Orchestra.'

'Of course we're going, then, if you really want to, but do you feel like driving, dear girl? I'd better call a cab.'

'Absolutely not—I'm perfectly able to drive. Please don't fuss, Mike.'

He was visibly hurt. 'My apologies,' he said quietly. 'I'd forgotten for the moment how very independent you are.'

It wouldn't be much of an evening if they went on like

this—not to mention playing Fran's game for her. Yona pulled herself together, apologised beautifully, told him she didn't know what had come over her and he must be wishing he was taking out almost anybody but her.

It was wonderful to see how quickly he responded. 'You could get round the most hardened misogynist,' he said indulgently, kissing her cheek. He had aimed for her mouth, but she'd moved at the wrong moment. 'Do you always get your own way?' he whispered.

'You surely don't expect me to confess to that,' she returned archly, to find herself engulfed in his arms again, and this time his kiss found its mark. 'I'm putty in your hands,' he claimed.

And not only in *my* hands, thought Yona unwillingly, visited again by the morning's sightings. 'How is Dr Melling?' she asked as a result.

'Doc Melling?' asked Mike with surprise as he released her. 'He's fine. Why?'

Bang went the idea that he'd only been comforting Fran over-thoroughly that morning. 'Oh, I just wondered,' she claimed with false lightness, 'when his daughter is rarely away from his side.' Or yours!

'But that's the way she is, Yona—devoted to a fault. I told you. And now we really must be going...'

In the foyer of the splendid Salchester Symphonic Hall, Yona was cheered and partially reassured by the evident pride in Mike's voice as he introduced her to some friends of his, a young married couple. He was making no attempt to hide his interest in her. And not a word was said about the dreaded Fran, she thought gratefully as they asked Mike to bring Yona to see them and he accepted with flattering speed.

'Did you like my friends the Westons?' asked Mike as they settled in their seats.

'Yes, very much. I thought they were charming.'

'Good! We'll visit them this coming weekend, then. They're a perfect example of—' He broke off as the conductor came onto the platform to a burst of applause. 'Wedded bliss,' Mike hissed in her ear in the quiet moment before the concert began. A remark like that could take her mind off both the music and Fran, if anything could. Because if Mike wanted to show her his idea of wedded bliss, then was she not the foolish one to worry? Unconsciously, she leaned nearer to him, savouring the feel of his arm against hers.

Mike felt it, too, and reached out to cover her clasped hands with his warm brown one for a moment. How silly I am to doubt him, she decided, relaxing and letting the wonderful music wash over her. She couldn't remember the last time she'd felt as happy as this.

'So, what's your verdict on the famous SSO, then?' asked Mike as they shuffled with the crowd out into the cold of the night when the concert was over.

'Magnificent! They certainly deserve their reputation.'

'So perhaps Salchester is not such a dreary, ugly, old dump after all.'

'It's ugly all right,' said Yona, 'but it's got lots of good points as well.'

'Tell me!' he invited.

'Well, all that for a start.' She waved a hand backwards to take in the hall and the orchestra. 'Some very nice people—and, of course, the botanic gardens. Especially on a wet Sunday afternoon...'

Mike seized her round the waist and kissed her, despite the crowd. 'You'll not forget Sunday in a hurry then, huh?'

'Absolutely not—my best jacket got shrunk!'

'And is that *all* that happened that day?' he asked softly.

Yona couldn't help remembering a tearful Fran on her doorstep. 'It started better than it ended,' she reminded him.

'But we've made up for that since,' Mike insisted. 'And this is how it's going to be for us from now on.' He swept her across the road into a packed wine bar.

'We'll never get a table,' said Yona, looking round.

'Pessimist,' Mike accused her fondly. 'I've already booked a table away from the crowd. Come on!'

'You certainly know your way around,' she said approvingly as he towed her up the stairs.

'Which is why you find me irresistible,' he retorted.

'Do I?' she asked, although pretty sure he was right.

'It'd be a great pity if you didn't—considering the way I feel about you!'

'And what way is that, then?' asked Yona when they were seated in a nice quiet little corner.

'Actions speak louder than words, but if I were to show you here the waiter would fetch a policeman or a bucket of water. What would you like to eat?'

'Eat?' she echoed, swamped by the wave of desire his words had provoked. Heavens—he didn't even need to touch her! 'Eat, you said... Oh, spaghetti, please.'

'Are you sure?'

'This is an Italian place, is it not?'

'Well spotted, but the menu is a mile long and very imaginative. Don't you want to see it?'

The only thing Yona wanted to see at that moment was Mike Preston naked in her arms, in her bed. 'I'd rather you chose,' she managed faintly.

'Then things *are* looking up,' he decided, before telling the waiter, 'The lady wants spaghetti, Guiseppe—with some of Marcello's special sauce.'

By the time they'd eaten, Yona was feeling calmer. She was thinking again, too. Mike fancied her—that much was obvious—and she wanted him more than she'd ever wanted any man, but nothing had really been changed by this wonderful evening. Fran was still there—a shadowy third—and there she'd stay until Yona was absolutely certain that the old ties were broken and Mike was free.

'You've gone all solemn again,' he said as they went to get his car.

'Have I? I expect that's because I'm a bit tired.' Quite true, tired of wondering and worrying...

'And I know the best cure for that,' he whispered, drawing her closer.

'So do I—eight hours' sleep.' If only she didn't feel it necessary to keep him at arm's length like this...

'That's one way, I suppose,' he allowed, 'but definitely not what I had in mind.'

His arm round her waist, with his hand just below her breast, was playing havoc with her resolve. 'Have you ever slept with Fran?' she asked jerkily, surprising herself as well as Mike.

'Have I *what*?' He sounded scandalised. 'What the hell will you come out with next? Are you crazy?'

'No—but I am curious.' She most definitely was, so they may as well get things out in the open now she'd started. 'You've known her for ever and she worships you. It was a—reasonable assumption.'

'No, it damn well wasn't—and you should have known it!'

'Because Fran's not that sort of girl?'

'Because she doesn't attract me—and never has.'

'I suppose it is possible to like somebody—even be fond of them—without wanting to...to...'

'Sleep with them? Of course it is! Just as it's possible to fancy somebody you don't like.'

'But you wouldn't know about that,' said Yona.

'Would you?'

'We're not talking about me, we're—'

'And why not? I'm as keen to find out about your views and standards as you are to suss out mine,' he said tightly.

'But I'm not juggling two men at once!' snapped Yona.

'If you say so!' he snapped back as Yona unlocked the car.

They drove home in a fraught and angry silence and Mike was out of the car almost before Yona had brought it to a stop in the underground garage at the flats. Then he leaned down to say, 'A relationship without trust is not worth having. Think about that!' He slammed the door with a force that rocked the heavy car, leaving Yona to watch him limp over to the lift, get in and disappear. Then she got out, locked the car and took the other lift to her own part of the building. She was stiff with misery.

After work the next day, Friday, Yona went to the supermarket near the flats to stock up for the week. She spotted Angie Bertram, Mike's next-door neighbour and Fran's devoted friend, queuing at the next checkout. The look she gave Yona was so murderous as to freeze the beginning of a smile on Yona's face. Thank heaven it's not me she lives next door to, thought Yona with a little shiver. I'd need to get the flat bomb-proofed.

To avoid a direct confrontation, Yona pretended to have forgotten something and went round the store again. Even so, she drove into the garage only seconds after Angie.

Again there was that murderous glance as their eyes met and then Angie came storming over. 'I hope you're proud of yourself!' she snarled.

Yona blinked in the face of such fury. 'And I hope you know what you mean by that, for I'm sure I don't!' she retorted bravely.

'Oh, very cool! But, then, your sort always is—or you wouldn't get away with it!'

'Get away with what?' asked Yona, although she could see now what Angie was driving at.

'Ruining people's lives—that's what! I always said he wasn't good enough for her, but he's what she wants and they were perfectly all right until *you* came. But your turn will come. His sort doesn't know how to be faithful!' Then she turned and stamped off towards the lifts before Yona could say another word. Just as well. Yona had no idea how to deal with such a hysterical outburst in somebody who wasn't a patient.

She thinks she's put me down, but wouldn't she be mad if she knew that she's actually cheered me up? thought Yona, going for the lift herself. She'd never have gone for me like that unless Mike really has put an end to Fran's hopes. She quickened her steps, desperate to see him and patch up last night's silly quarrel.

Once in her flat she dumped her shopping and went to the phone, but Mike's number was engaged. Trying again three minutes later, she got no reply. There was nothing for it but to put a note through his door. She scribbled a few disjointed lines, appealing for a meeting, and dashed out of the flat.

Mike stepped out of the lift as she rushed past it to the stairs. He called after her. She turned round, her heart thumping, and they stared at one another.

'I rang, but your number was engaged,' he said.

'I rang you—and so was yours.' They started to laugh as they realised how that had happened. Then they both started forward and fell into one another's arms, murmuring apologies between kisses until the whirring of the lift suggested an imminent audience. They made for the privacy of Yona's flat and as she shut them in Mike came straight to the point, asking, 'What went wrong last night?'

'I'd seen you outside the surgical block with Fran that morning—and you looked extremely friendly.'

'You silly girl,' he said tenderly.

'And as Ted keeps referring to Dr Melling as your prospective father-in-law, then—'

'Oh, does he?' Mike frowned. 'Then the sooner I set him straight, the better. I did tell Fran, you know. You've got to believe me!'

'But what exactly did you tell her, Mike?'

'That I've only ever thought of her as a friend and that I'm now seriously attracted to you.'

'Plain enough, I'd have thought,' said Yona, while wondering why that seemed less than enough.

'Then why aren't you looking more cheerful?' he asked perceptively.

'Angie Bertram went for me in the garage tonight,' she said, rather than answer him directly.

'That figures. As I told you, she and Fran go way back.' He paused. 'You said she went for you. Surely you don't mean she physically attacked you?'

'Only with words. Among other things, she told me it would soon be my turn to be dumped as your sort is notoriously unfaithful.'

Mike found that extremely funny and his burst of laughter echoed round the living room.

'Can I take it that you haven't left a string of bleeding hearts along the way, then?' asked Yona when he'd calmed down.

'If I have, nobody told me,' he answered. 'There have been girls, of course, but, as I told you, nobody I felt seriously about—and Fran was definitely not one of them.

And don't tell me it hasn't been a bit like that for you, too, because I wouldn't believe you!'

'So we're starting more or less level, then,' said Yona.

'Never mind the start—it's the finish that interests me,' said Mike firmly, as he pulled her close with the usual unnerving results.

'Leave it,' he murmured when the phone rang soon after.

'I can't,' she said. 'It might be important.' Besides, she still couldn't rid herself of the idea that bed might be all he was interested in.

It was Meg Burnley on the line, wanting to know if Yona would like to spend Sunday with them if she'd nothing better to do.

'Thank you—that would be lovely, Meg,' she said, wondering if Ted had put her up to it in order to sort out his new assistant away from the hospital.

'What would you have me do?' she asked when Mike said she should have refused. 'Her husband is my boss after all. Besides, I love their company.'

'It's just that I'd told the Westons that we'd go to see them on Sunday. But, no matter, we'll go there tomorrow instead.'

'If it suits them.'

'Oh, it'll suit them,' he said easily. 'They're always glad to see me.'

'With your current female in tow?'

It was out before she knew what she was going to say, and he suspected her of needling him again. 'With or without,' he returned evenly. 'And I'm not going to quarrel with you again—no matter how much you provoke me. Though I really don't know why you want to.'

'I think I must be hungry,' said Yona, hoping she sounded pathetic. 'I didn't have time for lunch today.'

'Come to think of it, neither did I,' he said. 'Get your coat on—we're going over the road to Le Café du Parc.'

There, as on Monday, they had another good and unpretentious meal—and with no Angie there to curdle the milk this time. But Mike was not disposed to linger and he told the waiter they wouldn't be wanting coffee. 'Your place or mine?' he asked as they returned to the flats.

'That depends,' said Yona thoughtfully.

'On what?' he asked predictably.

'On which of us makes the best coffee?' she suggested after a tiny pause.

'You think I'm pushing too hard, don't you?' he asked acutely.

'Let's just say I'd not want you to run away with the idea that I'm just anybody's in return for a good dinner,' she admitted candidly.

She was sorry the minute she'd said it because the look in his eyes told her more plainly than words that she'd hit him hard.

'Oh, Mike—I'm so sorry! I didn't mean—'

'I think you did,' he interrupted quietly but forcefully, 'but you needn't worry. If I thought you were like that, I'd not want any more to do with you. The Nonie Burkes of this world hold no attraction for me.'

'Now I feel dreadful,' she said, both sounding and looking it.

'Good—that's how I meant you to feel,' he said. 'Shall I come up with you, or would you rather I went straight home?'

'Please come up. I'd really like it if you would,' she said earnestly.

So Yona made coffee and they talked, learning more about each other, like any two fairly newly acquainted people. At first. Inevitably, as the evening wore on, the space between them on Yona's comfy sofa got smaller and smaller until Mike could slip his arm around her shoulders. 'This is perfect,' he whispered. 'Don't you dare to tell me that it isn't.'

'I can't,' she whispered back, because it was. And wasn't she a fool to hold back—not to trust him? What was the matter with her? 'You can stay if you like,' she whispered, thrilled at the answering fire in his eyes and then absurdly disappointed when after a momentary tightening of his arms around her body he drew away with a smothered groan and got awkwardly to his feet.

'If you say that to me the next time we're alone like this, I'll know you really mean it,' he said emotionally. 'God knows, the last thing I want is to pressure you into something you're not sure about. 'I'll ring you in the morning.'

He was gone almost before she'd realised he intended to leave.

As Mike had promised, he phoned Yona at nine next morning and arranged to pick her up at twelve. They were going to see the Westons.

'Is it far?' she asked when he'd directed her onto the city bypass.

'About four miles,' he returned. 'Just watch for a sign saying Griston Village.'

Hearing that, Yona expected something quaint in the country, but Griston had long ago been swallowed up by the city and the Westons lived in a modern house in a well-kept suburban street lined with grass and trees.

They, their three children and a contented-looking cat were lined up on the front step, waiting to welcome their guests.

Mike was obviously a great favourite with all the children, but the eldest—a boy—soon turned his attention to

Yona. 'I thought you were Scotch,' he said, sounding disappointed.

'So I am,' she agreed. Billy was too young to know the difference between Scotch and Scots.

'But you're not wearing a kilt,' he reproved her severely.

'Girls only wear kilts for dancing,' she explained with a smile.

'That's not true,' said Billy firmly. 'My granny's got one. Can you play the bagpipes, then?'

'I'm afraid not,' she owned, sorry to be such a disappointment. 'But I can make Scotch pancakes—and I've seen the Loch Ness monster.'

'You haven't! Honest?' Her credibility as a Scot was restored.

'Cross my heart,' promised Yona. 'Mind you, my dad told me it was only a bit of an old tree, but I knew he was wrong. My brother saw it too.'

'She's seen Nessie! She's seen Nessie!' cried Billy, running into the house.

'You said the right thing there, Yona,' said Mary Weston, laughing. 'He's monster-mad and now there'll be no peace until we promise to take him to see it.'

'Maybe it wasn't the right thing, then,' suggested Yona, as Billy came rushing up to her with his bendy rubber monster. 'Yes, that's just how she looked, Billy, but she's ever so shy, you know. She hides if she thinks somebody is looking.'

'Mummy, can we—?'

'Yes, of course, darling—in the summer holidays. It wouldn't be a problem, not now we've got the caravan,' she assured Yona. 'It's the best way, really, with children. People aren't always kind to them in hotels.'

'Hardly a holiday for you, though,' surmised Yona.

'I love it,' claimed Mary. 'And John is very good about sharing the chores.'

'Mary adores her children,' Mike whispered in Yona's ear. 'And you've made a great hit with Billy. Well done!'

The pre-lunch drinks and the meal itself were all children-orchestrated, but afterwards John and Mike took them to play in the gardens while Yona helped Mary to clear away and wash up.

'Could you not do with a dishwasher?' asked Yona, thinking of the one in her little flat.

'It would be nice,' Mary admitted, 'but somehow there's always something needed for the children—and, anyway, I'm not exactly pressed for time.'

'You don't work, then?' Even as she asked, Yona realised what a silly question it was when Billy was the only one of school age.

Mary looked shocked. 'Oh, no! We'd always agreed that I'd give up when the children came—and so I did.'

'What did you do?' asked Yona, thinking it couldn't have been anything particularly exciting. 'I hope you weren't too keen,' she added, in case her question had sounded rather blunt.

'I was an infant teacher—and I loved it,' said Mary. 'But you can't have everything, can you? Not if you're a woman and a mother.'

No wonder Mike thinks the Westons are the perfect married couple, Yona found herself thinking. Mary is another Meg Burnley. 'That depends,' she said. 'Some jobs can't just be laid aside and picked up again years later when you feel like it. Mine, for instance.'

'Oh, I don't know,' Mary disagreed. 'Meg managed it. You know Meg Burnley, don't you? She went back half-time in school clinics as soon as their youngest started secondary school.'

Yona wondered if Mary understood the difference between routine basic inspections and high-tech specialised hospital medicine. 'And then she took a refresher course and now she's in general practice,' Mary added.

'So I understand. Your children are gorgeous—and so friendly and well behaved,' offered Yona, moving onto safer ground.

'Yes, they are good children, though I say it myself,' agreed Mary proudly. 'John says it's because they feel so secure with Mummy always here for them.'

'I think you're marvellous,' said Yona, really meaning that. 'I'm not sure I could be that unselfish.'

'Wait till you have your first one,' remarked Mary confidently, 'and then you'll soon see that selfishness doesn't come into it.'

When the dishes had been washed and put away, Mary took Yona into the garden to find the others. It was clear that the lives of both Westons revolved around their children and Yona wondered how they'd managed to get to the concert on Thursday evening.

'No problem,' answered Mary when Yona put the question. 'Fortunately, we live quite near to both sets of grandparents and they vie with each other to babysit. In fact, we'd be out every night if they had their way.' She broke off to call, 'Billy, stop that! You know Lucy hates getting her feet wet.'

'She'll be getting more than her feet wet soon—and so will all of us,' reckoned Mike, squinting up at a huge black cloud coming in fast from the west.

'Does it always rain at the weekends in Salchester?' asked Yona when they were indoors again.

'Only when I'm off,' said Mike. 'I can safely promise you that the next one will be a scorcher.'

When the children grew tired of watching the rain

bounce off the patio, Billy asked Yona to show him how to make pancakes. Mary thought that was a wonderful idea so they all piled into the kitchen to watch.

The results were less than perfect, but they all got eaten at teatime.

Baths came next, and then the children's supper. 'I've never known a day pass so quickly,' said Yona, feeling quite tired when the last small Weston had finally fallen asleep.

When Mike said they really ought to be going, Mary wouldn't hear of them going without their supper.

'Have you enjoyed your day?' asked Mike when he and Yona were finally on their way back to the city centre just the right side of midnight.

'Very much,' she said. 'Such a lovely family—and Mary is a saint.'

'A very happy saint,' said Mike with a smile.

'Oh, Lord, yes—anybody can see that. She reminds me a bit of Meg Burnley.'

'Two perfect women,' he said firmly.

Well, he would think that, wouldn't he?

'Don't you agree?' he persisted.

'They're both obviously happy and contented,' she admitted.

'That's because they're both fulfilled.'

'You could be right,' she allowed, determined not to provoke another row—about anything. 'We turn off at the next set of lights, if I'm not mistaken...'

'You've got a very good sense of direction—for a woman,' Mike said indulgently.

'Thank you kindly, oh master,' Yona couldn't help replying. 'That'll come in handy if I ever find myself in general practice.'

'Meg's in general practice now—just part time, of course. Did you know that?'

'Yes. She told me so herself.'

'And she loves it.'

'She told me that, too.'

'What's the matter, Yona?' he asked when she'd parked the car in the garage at the flats.

'Nothing,' she insisted. 'Nothing at all. I think your friends the Westons are quite delightful.'

'More or less what you said earlier. And I'm so glad you were impressed. Something to aim at, wouldn't you say?' he asked softly, leaning across and pulling her close to be kissed long and lingeringly.

But Yona's mind was filling with doubts and her response was rather less warm than usual. After a few moments Mike said, 'Something tells me that you'll not be inviting me in tonight.'

'You're very perceptive—for a man,' she said. 'Actually, I've got some thinking to do.'

'So have I,' he said, surprising her. 'Let's hope we both come up with the right answers.'

Yona watched him walk awkwardly away in that clumsy plaster and her heart ached with longing. But was just wanting enough? She wasn't jealous of Fran any more, but could she be the sort of woman Mike so obviously wanted? She loved her work—it was desperately important to her. Giving it up would be like losing a limb.

Why the hell did he have to be so confoundedly old-fashioned?

CHAPTER NINE

'I'M REALLY sorry to land you with this,' said Ted for the third time over lunch the following Wednesday. He'd told Yona first thing that morning that he'd been summoned to an emergency meeting of the university court, which meant she'd have to manage without him at the afternoon's follow-up clinic.

'I honestly don't mind,' Yona repeated. 'You can't help it and it'll do Charlie good to get a bit of responsibility.'

'I feel bad about it all the same,' Ted insisted, getting up to go. 'Especially when you're looking so tired after a busy night on.'

If Yona looked tired, it was less to do with night duty—which had been light for once—and more because of worry about her personal life. She'd neither seen nor heard from Mike since they'd parted after their visit to the Westons last Saturday.

They'd agreed that some thinking was required—but this much? Each day that passed made it harder to decide how to bridge the gap.

'I *always* see the professor,' said the first patient of the afternoon, looking around as though expecting Ted to pop out of a cupboard.

'Sorry, Mrs Murphy,' said Yona, 'but he's at the university this afternoon.'

'Whatever for?' wondered the old lady, as though that was the last place a respectable professor ought to be visiting.

'Academic business,' Yona explained firmly. 'Now, tell me how you've been keeping since your last visit.'

Mrs Murphy had nothing significant to report. She wasn't the only patient to resent Ted's absence, although Mr Robinson did allow that Yona was probably doing her best.

'That was some marathon,' Yona remarked thankfully to the nurse when she thought the clinic was over.

'I'm afraid you've still got two more to see, Doctor,' returned the nurse. 'A couple of surgical follow-ups who can't manage to get to the regular clinic.'

'Does Mr Preston know about this?' Yona asked carefully.

'Yes—he arranged it—but I'm told he's been delayed.'

'All right, let's get the first one in, then—at least I can check on her medical condition.'

'Remember me, Doctor?' asked young Karen, the prospective bride who'd been so keen to get her hip replacement before her wedding.

'I certainly do,' Yona answered with a big smile of welcome. 'And there's no need to ask if you're feeling the improvement. I can tell right away from your walking.'

'And it's not just my walking that's better, Doctor,' confided Karen with a saucy wink. 'Roy can get at me ever so much easier now.'

'I can guess.' Yona was chuckling as Mike tapped briefly on the door and came in.

'Where's Ted?' he asked when he saw Yona alone at the desk.

'Not you, too,' she sighed. 'Patients have been asking me that all afternoon. He's got a meeting at the university.'

'Too bad,' he returned briefly, before turning his attention to Karen. 'So, how's it going, then, young lady?'

'Wonderful, Doctor. I was just telling Dr MacFarlane how much easier Roy's finding it.'

Mike frowned heavily. 'It's only a month since your op, Karen—I hope the high jinks haven't been too energetic.'

'Oh, no—we both remembered what you told us.'

'Everything seems to be OK,' said Mike when he'd examined her, 'but we'd better have a check X-ray—just to make sure. When's the wedding?'

'On Saturday week. Will you be able to come, Doctor?'

Mike said he'd have to see about that. 'Isn't that a lot sooner than you told us, though?' he asked.

'Yes—but, what with getting my op so soon and then getting the chance of a nice ground-floor flat, we thought we may as well bring it forward.'

Mike gave her another warning, spelling out the consequences of dislocating her new hip. 'Just don't get carried away, that's all,' he wound up.

Karen promised faithfully to remember his warning.

'Do you really think she will remember?' asked Yona when Karen had gone.

'If she doesn't then she'll be very sorry—and I'll be furious,' he answered grimly.

'Of course, but newly marrieds... It is asking rather a lot.'

Mike cocked a derisive eyebrow. 'That's not what I'd have expected from you,' he said reproachfully.

'And I'd have thought you'd be more sympathetic.'

'I'm very sympathetic. I'm also more aware than you seem to be of the disastrous consequences of dislocating that hip. It's a great pity that Ted wasn't here to put the brakes on. She listens to him.'

'That's precisely why I told her to come back next week,' Yona told him crisply.

'Next week could be too late,' he answered doggedly.

'Why did you not admit her, then?'

'I almost wish I had,' he told her. 'Who's next?'

'Mrs Norma Brown—knee replacement. You saw her first back in March—on my first day here,' she recalled. 'Almost two months ago,' she murmured, half to herself.

'Is that all? It seems much longer,' Mike remarked. 'Ah, there you are, Mrs Brown. So, how's it going?'

'Just wonderful, Mr Preston. It's glorious to be pain-free.'

It was soon apparent that she'd made a textbook recovery, but Mike wanted to see her again in six weeks' time. 'Or sooner, if you have any problems,' he added.

'I'm sure there won't be,' she said confidently, 'but anything you say. I'm fair delighted with it—and so grateful.'

'Then it's all been worthwhile,' he told her, with one of his special smiles.

An awkward silence fell when Nurse had ushered Mrs Brown out and Mike and Yona were left alone. Has his thinking been as chaotic and useless as mine, then? she wondered with her eyes fixed anxiously on Mike's strong profile as he bent over the notes he was making. She only just managed to be looking elsewhere when he looked up.

'Well, that's it,' he said gruffly. 'Just one or two things to check in the wards and then I can go home.'

'Same here,' agreed Yona, before suggesting offhandedly, 'I could give you a lift if you like—to save you getting a taxi…'

'Thank you, but I hired an automatic yesterday,' he told her in the same gruff way. 'Can't think why I didn't think of it before.'

'Perhaps you had other things on your mind,' Yona suggested, but too late.

Mike had left the room with a brief 'Be seeing you.'

Was this the end of their fraught whirlwind relationship? It certainly seemed so and Yona knew she ought to be glad when there was nothing between them but a strong physical attraction. Even their shared profession divided rather than united them as Mike had such a violent dislike of successful career-women. 'Who'd be a woman?' she burst out, just as the cleaner came in, dragging a heavy vacuum cleaner.

'Nobody with any sense, love, and that's a fact,' she responded. 'Me, I'm coming back as a man—or else a dog with a good home, like our Tozer.'

'That's the first sensible thing I've heard from anybody all day,' Yona told her from the heart. 'Well, goodnight, Mrs Finch—and thank you for cheering me up!'

Mike left the hospital before Yona did. She knew that because from a window on her unit she saw him go. There was no sign of Fran today—as if that made any difference.

She turned back to her patient. 'As I told you earlier, Mr Potts, that was just a mild bout of indigestion—and definitely not anything the matter with your heart, so don't you be losing any sleep over it.'

'It's more likely this damn knee that'll be keeping me awake, Doctor,' he said.

'Then for goodness' sake don't be so obstinate about taking the painkillers—you need your sleep. I shall leave a note for the night staff about that. Right?'

'Right, Doctor. You're the boss—except when Sister's about,' he added with a sly wink.

Lying on Yona's hall floor when she got home, along with the usual daily ration of junk mail, she found a neatly folded note.

'If you want to talk, I'll be in all evening,' it ran. 'If not, I'll not be pressuring you. I've done too much of that already. Mike.'

She leaned against the wall, weak with relief. He didn't want to end it—he wanted them to continue. What else could it mean?

Her first instinct was to rush round straight away and fling herself into his arms the minute he opened the door, but he'd suggested talking—something they'd not been terribly good at so far. Better to wait and get her thoughts straight first...

She popped a ready snack meal from Marks & Spencer in the oven and took a shower while it was heating up. She was just sitting down to eat when the phone rang. She sensed who was calling before she picked it up.

'Just wondering if you got my note,' Mike said gruffly.

'Yes, I... Yes. I was just going to ring...'

'You were late getting home,' he assumed.

'Later than you, I guess...' Why couldn't she think of something sparkling to say?

'Have you eaten?' he was asking.

'No, not yet. I—'

'I've got enough for two here—if you're interested.'

'Sounds great,' said Yona, even though he hadn't told her what he was offering.

'I'll keep it hot, then,' said Mike, sounding relieved.

Yona leapt up from the table, grabbed her keys and made for the door, then backtracked to brush her hair and take the shine off her nose. Then she looked round for something to take and found a jar of peaches in brandy.

'My contribution to the feast,' she said, holding it out to him as he opened the door.

'You didn't need to,' he said, 'but thanks anyway...' He stood aside to let her in.

'May I offer you a drink?' he asked formally as he ushered her into his living room.

Yona said that a small dry sherry would be lovely.

Mike poured two dry sherries and sat down when she did, though not too close to her.

'This is nice,' she said desperately after a moment.

'A present from a grateful patient,' he told her, thinking she meant the sherry.

They talked earnestly about patients, grateful and otherwise, until Mike said he'd better go and look in the oven.

After a minute Yona followed him to the kitchen. 'In case I can help to carry things,' she explained.

'I was just going to call you,' he said, and she noticed that the table was already set. 'It saves all the trailing to and fro if we eat here,' he added. 'I hope you don't mind.'

'Of course not—it's very kind of you to—to entertain when you're hampered by that wretched plaster.'

'It's no trouble,' he said. 'I have to eat anyway...'

They ate a selection of baby vegetables with a delicious beef casserole which was definitely home-made and Yona wondered where he'd got it.

'You're a very good cook,' she offered afterwards, as a way of finding out.

'Any fool can follow a recipe,' he said, but he sounded pleased all the same.

'I've known plenty of reasonably bright folk who couldn't—me included,' she admitted.

'I don't believe that,' said Mike. 'It seems to me that you generally succeed at anything you want to.'

'Far from it,' denied Yona, thinking what a mess she'd helped to make of their relationship so far. 'Anyway, is that so bad—to be fairly successful?'

'How could it be?' asked Mike unhelpfully.

'You tell me,' she invited gently. 'After all, we are supposed to be—be talking...'

'And bloody difficult it's turning out to be!' he exploded, breaking the ice and making them both laugh.

'Oh, Yona—what fools we are,' he said when they'd calmed down a bit.

'Pathetic, I call it,' was her opinion. 'We spend all day sorting out others and yet we can't sort out ourselves.'

'Don't you be so sure,' he warned, getting up and lumbering round the table to pull Yona to her feet.

As always, his lightest touch was enough to prompt ripples of desire. It was heavenly to be in his arms again and her response was the warmest ever after the anxiety of the past few days. 'Almost worth falling out for,' she murmured ecstatically.

'Oh, my darling...' He kissed her again, moving her towards the door.

In the bedroom he undressed her with a controlled yet eager care that drove her wild. She was ready and aching to receive him long before he judged her ready, and when he finally found his way to the place where he and only he would ever be welcome, Yona thought she would die of the joy of it. And when the storm was past and he lay spent and happy in her arms, she clutched him as tightly as ever, reluctant to let him go. He was her joy, her love, her life.

They were wakened just before midnight by the urgent ringing of the phone. Mike had to stretch across Yona to reach it. In seconds he was fully awake and out of bed, searching for his clothes.

'I didn't know you were on call,' she whispered, bewildered.

'I'm not, my darling, there's a major alert on. An air crash.' He bent down to kiss her and tell her to go back to sleep. 'I'll ring you first chance I get,' he promised. Then he grabbed a sweater and made for the door.

Yona woke next at her usual time, wondering where she was and why her body felt so relaxed and contented—until she remembered. She closed her eyes again, reliving those wonderful moments.

But where was Mike? Then she remembered too about the accident. She'd better not be late this morning—there could be repercussions even on her own unit if too many beds needed to be found.

She showered and dried herself with Mike's towels. They smelled faintly of him and she'd have liked to have stayed longer, hugging them around her. She ate cereal at the cluttered table they'd abandoned in such desperate haste the night before. It took Yona five minutes to clear the lot into the dishwasher. Then she stepped out onto the landing, just as Angie was putting out a note for the milkman.

She looked at Yona with undisguised hatred. 'This is going to break Fran's heart,' she hissed.

'If you think that then don't tell her,' retorted Yona, sounding calmer than she felt. In truth, she felt very sorry for Fran, but denying her own happiness because of Fran's unrealistic hopes made no sense. Besides, she was beginning to worry about Mike. He hadn't phoned her, as he'd said he would. Where was he? Was he all right? Sometimes the rescue and emergency teams called to major disasters were as much in danger as those directly involved.

There was an unmistakable air of drama at the hospital that morning, with more folk than usual in corridors and waiting rooms, hastily dressed and sleepless, waiting anxiously for news, while the staff—already frantically busy—rushed about with cups of tea for them.

On the rheumatic unit, Charlie had already compiled a list of patients who could, if absolutely necessary, be discharged to make room for emergencies.

'Do you know exactly what happened?' Yona asked as she scanned it.

'A plane crashlanded at the airport—they don't know why yet. Most of the passengers and crew got out, but there were many casualties. The General Hospital got most of them being nearest, but between thirty and forty were brought here.'

'Good God—what a calamity!' Yona had never before been even remotely involved with something of this scale. She turned back to Charlie's list. 'Not Mr Davies—his back is unstable. And not Mrs Dawson—she's only just completed her four weeks' total bed rest. I suppose Mr McCarthy could go at a pinch, although we've not got all his results yet... Surely it makes more sense to delay non-urgent admissions, Charlie?'

'Sure, but general orders for major incidents say do this—so that's what I'm doing.'

Yona found a ballpoint. 'I'm starring four who could go home if absolutely necessary, but don't do anything until the prof's given the OK— Oh, here you are, Ted. Have you heard the news?'

'I caught it on the car radio on the way here,' he returned. 'All the surgeons will have been called in, no doubt.'

'Yes, they have been,' Yona confirmed unguardedly. 'Two of them actually live in my block, don't forget,' she added before anybody could ask her how she knew.

Ted then agreed about their choice of patients, and they settled back into their usual, less demanding routine.

It was lunchtime before Yona saw Mike, and then only briefly in the corridor outside Theatre as she took a short cut to see if a rheumatic patient in Orthopaedics, recently operated on, could be discharged if necessary.

Mike looked tired and his blue cotton theatre clothes were stained and crumpled. 'Just taking a breather while waiting for clean things to arrive,' he explained. 'We've gone through the entire stock up here.'

'It must have been hectic.'

'That's putting it mildly,' he said. 'At times like this I

almost wish I'd chosen medicine. Dermatology, say. There can't be many emergencies in— Coming, Sister,' he said over his shoulder when someone called out that the laundry had turned up trumps.

He bent down to kiss the top of Yona's head. 'See you as soon as I possibly can, darling,' he whispered, before disappearing again.

He's optimistic, she thought, continuing her errand. He's on call tonight. And not a word about last night but, then, how could he? Not in a busy hospital corridor...

It was well after nine o'clock before Mike rang Yona's doorbell, and by then her carefully prepared dinner was past its best.

'Oh, honey, you shouldn't have waited,' he said contritely. 'I snatched a sandwich earlier—between jobs,' he added.

'That's all right, then,' she said, thinking that surely he could have phoned...

'No, it isn't,' he denied. 'Not when you'd gone to so much trouble. I picked up the phone more than once, only to be interrupted.'

'It sounds as though you've had a truly terrible day,' said Yona, thinking now how unreasonable *she* was being.

'I can't remember anything to touch it,' he said. 'Anyway, things are more or less stable now so I thought I'd dash home and see you—if only for a minute. Besides, I badly need a shower and a change of clothes.'

'Why not shower here while I fetch you some fresh things?' she suggested.

'Darling, you are wonderful,' he said gratefully, handing over his keys.

There was no angry Angie hovering on the doorstep tonight and Yona was back home in minutes. Mike had already showered and was prowling round her flat, draped inadequately in towels which he promptly threw aside when she handed him some Y-fronts.

The sight of his magnificent naked body was almost too much for Yona. 'It's a good thing you're on call,' she murmured from under lowered lashes.

'I call it damn bad luck,' he said with a wicked grin. 'All the same—' He was cut short by the phone. 'I hope that's not for me...'

But it was. 'Your registrar has just seen a complicated fracture of tib and fib he doesn't feel up to,' she reported.

'In my experience, he doesn't feel up to anything more exacting than a sprained ankle,' growled Mike, lumbering over to take the phone from her, still almost naked.

As he listened, his expression changed. 'Sounds a real corker,' he said, then went on, 'I'm sorry, but I'll have to go, my love. Lord, what a day!

'What a twenty-four hours, come to that,' he added softly—his first reference to their magical coming together the night before. He pulled her close and kissed her fit to melt her bones. 'I'm afraid that's the best I can do for now,' he said whimsically. 'What a good thing you're not also a surgeon, my darling, or we'd have even more of a problem in front of us.'

He was dressed and away before Yona could ask what he'd meant by that. She thought she could probably guess, though—and she hoped with all her heart that she was wrong.

'We're going to have to do something about the on-call,' Mike said firmly over lunch next day when he discovered that Yona was on call that night—and for the whole weekend.

'Like what?' she said. She couldn't see how the medical

registrars' rota could be made to fit in with that of the orthopaedic consultants.

'We'll think of something,' he said confidently. 'We can't have our love life upset like this.'

'Is that what you'll tell them when they ask you why you want things changed?' asked Yona, with an indulgent little smile.

'If necessary,' he insisted. 'Besides, it doesn't seem five minutes since you were on before. How is that?'

'We're a bit out of step at the moment, what with holidays and study leave,' she explained. 'It'll probably not work out quite as badly as this again.'

'I hope not for your sake, darling. All the same, you must admit it makes more sense for us both to be on call at the same time.'

'It would certainly be nicer,' she agreed. 'I just don't see how it can be arranged, though.'

'Do you realise it'll be Tuesday night now before we're both off?' he calculated, looking horrified.

'That's the way the cookie crumbles,' agreed Yona, eyeing the canteen clock. 'But I have to go now—a class of first-year nurses.'

'Couldn't you manage to sound a bit more upset?' grumbled Mike. 'I'm beginning to think that you don't fancy me as much as I fancy you.'

Yona sent him an intimate smile. 'If you can think that then you must have a very short memory,' she said softly, to be thrilled by the spark of fire her words evoked in his deep-set, expressive eyes. 'Dear one,' she went on, 'I'm as fed up as you are about this, but there's nothing we can do about it. Of course, if I were a consultant like you, I could be on call at home too.'

That made good sense to Yona, but she soon realised she'd said the wrong thing, judging by the way his mouth tightened. But she didn't have the time to try and put things right now.

'Darling, I have to go—eighteen eager young nurses are waiting to hear my words of wisdom. I'll phone you any spare second I get tonight—promise.' She kissed her fingertips and brushed his cheek with them in passing. 'You be a good boy, now,' she whispered.

'What choice do I have?' he asked glumly.

They didn't meet again until the combined clinic on Monday, and then, of course, Ted was there too—not to mention all the patients.

Karen was among them. Yona had already explained why she was there so Ted wasted no time in reinforcing what she'd heard from Mike the week before. 'We've done our bit and now it's up to you whether or not your new hip is a success,' he wound up. 'I hope you understand that, my girl?'

Karen said of course she did and she intended to be sensible. 'Do you want me to sign something?' she asked, sounding more like her usual perky self.

'That won't be necessary as we've got this conversation on tape,' said Ted, as he switched off the contraption on his desk.

'Well, I never,' breathed Karen. 'When you said you'd be recording our conversation, I thought you meant you were writing it down—like a police statement. See you at the wedding, then. You're still coming, aren't you?' she pleaded.

'Try and stop me,' said Ted, smiling.

When she'd gone Mike said thoughtfully, 'If a bright girl like that can misunderstand, we'd better revise our way of putting things—make sure that every patient understands clearly that all important conversations will be taped.'

Ted agreed and delivered one of his speeches about how

awful these modern times were when patients were encouraged on all sides to sue on the slimmest of grounds—and he really didn't know what the world was coming to!

'A full stop—just like this clinic will, if we don't get on with it,' said Mike with a grin. 'Yona, be a love and tell them to send in the next customer.'

Because I'm the junior or because I'm a woman? she wondered. Probably the latter. After all, the director of nursing had recently taken away a nurse from this clinic—because one of the doctors was a woman and would do as a chaperone!

It was a longer clinic than usual and Mike, being orthopaedic consultant on standby, was called away twice, stretching it out even more. Add on four new patients for Yona afterwards—all needing lengthy assessments—and she was very late getting home.

With Mike being on call that night, she had volunteered to cook supper. She went straight to the kitchen to rustle up something quick and easy.

He arrived before it was quite ready and lounged in the kitchen doorway, watching her at work. 'I love to see your domestic side,' he told her.

'And why is that?' she asked.

'Because there was a time when I was afraid you hadn't got one.'

'That's silly,' she told him. 'There are certain things everybody has to do for themselves if they're not to starve—or live like a pig.'

'I couldn't agree more in general, but right now you really seem to be enjoying yourself.'

'Why wouldn't I? After all, I'm cooking for the man I—who's tops with me right now.' She'd almost said the man I love, but she didn't mean to make such an admission before he did.

'So I'm on trial, then, am I?' he asked, sounding rattled.

'No more than I am, I guess. Taste this and tell me if it needs more salt.' She held out a spoonful of spaghetti sauce.

'It tastes wonderful,' he said. 'What's for pudding?'

'Some early strawberries, jazzed up with a spot of something out of a bottle.'

'And here was I hoping for apple pie,' he pretended jokingly. 'But, then, she'll be wanting to keep me wide awake and at peak performance…'

'What she doesn't want to do is to put him to sleep with too heavy a meal when he's on call.'

'Ah—but he isn't,' he said, advancing and embracing her from behind as she stood at the stove.

'Since when?' asked Yona, almost spilling the food at the touch of him.

'Since four o'clock this afternoon—when my opposite number begged me to change with him so that he could attend his child's school concert tomorrow, undisturbed.'

'So you'll be on when I'm off tomorrow,' said Yona.

'You're also off tonight,' he murmured, kissing the back of her neck.

'Off, yes—and thoroughly knackered after a hectic weekend on.'

'I'll soon cure that,' he whispered.

He did, too—and soon enough after they'd eaten to give them both indigestion, anybody would have thought. But, no—it was as wonderful as the first time, which was saying something. While we've got this, how can anything possible go wrong for us? wondered Yona as they finally settled to sleep in one another's arms.

The next month was the happiest time Yona had ever known. Somehow—she never quite understood how—Mike contrived to arrange that their on-calls almost always coincided. Even the weather was on their side, allowing them long, lazy days in the country at weekends, with a nice diet of concerts, plays and leisurely meals, in and out, during the week.

It wasn't long before their friends were saying they never knew which number to ring, but at least when you did get an answer you could be sure of getting both of them. They were an item—and everybody knew it.

And then came the Burnleys' silver wedding party.

When she realised they were having the party at home, Yona naturally offered her help, but Meg said she was getting caterers in and all Yona needed to do was to turn up, looking pretty.

Sister Evans had already collected for and bought the unit's present, but Yona and Mike wanted to give something just from themselves. It was sitting on Yona's dressing table now—a delightful little chafing dish, beautifully gift-wrapped and beribboned. They knew that Meg had a weakness for Georgian silver.

Yona kept glancing at it all the time she was dressing. It seemed to confirm what she still, in her heart, was afraid to accept. That this thing she and Mike had was real—and permanent.

She had bought a new dress for this party—a lovely creation of russet gold, which made the most of her figure and complemented her colouring perfectly. 'Not bad,' she told her reflection, before running eagerly to the door when she heard Mike's key in the lock.

He gazed at her as though he couldn't believe his luck. 'You're the most wonderful, beautiful thing I ever saw,' he said slowly. 'What have I done to deserve you?'

'Everything right so far—so keep it up,' she teased, happy as always just to see him. And then she noticed.

'Darling! You've got that ruddy plaster off at last! Is it all right? No pain? You must be so glad to be rid of the wretched thing!'

'Not at all,' he said. 'Kindly remember it brought us together—so I'm having it stuffed and mounted and given the place of honour in our new house, when we get it.'

Yona doubled up with laughter at such a prospect. 'Promise me you'll never change,' she begged when she'd calmed down. 'Nobody has ever made me laugh as much as you do.'

'Only if you promise me the same thing. Oh, Yona...'

'Oh, Mike... But we don't have time, my hero. We're going to be late as it is.'

And certainly the party was in full swing by the time they got there, and the lovely old house was packed with all the Burnley friends and colleagues, and relations from both sides of the family. Only the Burnleys' youngest son, who was taking a year out between school and college, was missing.

The caterers had wanted to put up a marquee in the garden, but Meg didn't trust the Salchester weather sufficiently for that so they'd opened the folding doors between the dining room and Ted's study for the buffet, and pre-food drinks were being served in the sitting room and hall. There was also a sizeable crowd in the kitchen, to the despair of the waiters.

Meg looked lovely and wonderfully happy in silvery grey and Ted had been persuaded into his best suit for the occasion. 'Find yourself a wife like mine—if you can,' he kept saying to all the people wanting to know his secret for a happy marriage.

Yona looked round for the Westons, but Mike said they'd probably not be coming as Billy had come down with measles and they were waiting for the others to copy him.

'Why haven't they all been immunised?' Yona asked practically.

'Because they don't believe in it,' he replied, 'and, of course, neither of them would come without the other. Now, let's go and get something to eat before it all disappears.'

The speeches came after supper and by far the most moving was Ted's tribute to 'my wonderful wife whose selfless devotion to her family was at the cost of her own promising career'.

At that, Yona felt tears pricking her eyelids, but she couldn't help telling Meg how much she agreed with everything Ted had said.

Meg looked quite surprised. 'When you've been happily married as long as I have, you'll understand what I mean when I say that a happy marriage is worth any dazzling career you could possibly think of,' she told Yona. 'Besides, we've always been a partnership. Now, where's the dean? He's told me three times how much he wants to meet your father's lovely daughter.'

Oh, dear, thought Yona, depressed at the thought of being labelled her father's daughter just when she'd thought she'd put all that behind her.

But the Dean of the Salchester Medical School had other things on his mind. 'Professor Burnley thinks very highly of your work, Dr MacFarlane,' he said when they'd been introduced at last.

Yona flushed with pleasure as she responded, 'Thank you very much, sir. Rheumatology has been my main interest since I was a student, and I consider myself very fortunate to be working with such an eminent consultant as Ted—Professor Burnley.'

'I'm also told that you like Salchester.'

'Yes, I do, sir—very much. I've made some wonderful friends here.'

'I've been hearing that, too—and here comes one of them now, if I'm not mistaken,' he said as Mike joined them, looking curious.

There were several minutes of general chat before the Dean turned his attention exclusively to Yona again. 'You'll have heard that we're considering the creation of a junior consultant post in your speciality at the General, Doctor—Yona, if I may.'

'Of course, sir. Yes, I had heard about that possibility.'

'You're already taking clinics there—and very satisfactorily, I'm told.'

Yona sensed a sudden stillness in Mike, so close beside her, and she felt afraid for no good reason that she could think of. 'Ted suggested that, and I was only too glad of the chance to enlarge my experience,' she explained. 'I hope there's no problem about that...'

'None at all,' he returned emphatically. 'As a matter of fact, it was my own idea—a little test, if you like. But enough of that for the time being—things are still only at the discussion stage, but I'm glad we've had this little talk. And now I mustn't keep you any longer from enjoying this delightful party.' Gracefully, he melted back into the crowd.

It had been very delicately done, but his meaning was clear. Yona was being seriously considered for the new junior consultant post.

His meaning had also been very clear to Mike. 'Why didn't you tell him straight out that you're not interested in a consultancy?' he asked bluntly.

'Because I am,' she told him just as bluntly. 'And I'm very flattered that he obviously thinks I'm up to it.'

'Of course you are, darling,' he allowed, 'and I'm very proud of you, but it's just not on, is it?'

'Are you going to tell me why?' asked Yona.

'Well, we've already agreed that we want children—which is why we're looking for a decent house with a good garden.'

'I'd not be the first woman to be a consultant *and* a mother,' she pointed out.

'Get real, Yona,' said Mike, torn between amusement and impatience. 'What sort of life would we have if you tried a juggling act like that?'

'A much better one than we'd have if I turned into a bored housewife!' she flashed.

'Why should you be bored?' he said. 'Meg's not bored. Mary's not bored—'

'And I'm not a Meg or a Mary—I'm me! And I love my work more than—more than—'

'More than you love me?' he asked dangerously.

'Don't be silly! And keep your voice down,' she implored. 'People are looking at us.'

For answer, he took her arm and towed her through the crowd and towards the comparative quiet of the garden. '*Do* you love your work more than you love me?' he asked again.

'You're putting words into my mouth,' she protested. 'And it's not fair! You seem to be saying that I must give up my work in order to marry you.'

'No, I am not—I'm not that reactionary. But something part time—something less demanding than hospital work. I don't want you wearing yourself out.'

'Be honest,' she challenged. 'Admit that what you don't want is a wife whose job is just as important as yours!' Yona was seething now. 'What's your objection? Are you afraid she'll outshine you? Grow up, for God's sake!'

'What I don't want is a wife who's never there for me or our children!' he thundered. 'Is that clear enough for you?'

'Oh, very clear—to me and to everybody within half a mile, I should think! It's plain to see that you don't want a wife with anything resembling a *mind*, Mike Preston! You just want a—a devoted doormat! So why don't you marry Fran? She's tailor-made for the job!'

After that they glared at one another for a long fraught minute. Then Mike said grimly, 'You know what? I'm beginning to think you're right!'

'I hope you'll both be very happy,' yelled Yona, before half running, half stumbling towards the house.

CHAPTER TEN

ONCE in the house, Yona went to hide in the cloakroom which was mercifully empty. She was shaking with rage. Mike was impossible, completely out of his time. What right had he to demand that she should make all the sacrifices? It made no more sense than it would if she were to tell him that he must put his career on hold! Compromise was the thing, but he wasn't capable of that. Her mind teemed with all the arguments she could have put forward, if only he hadn't hurt her so much with his draconian demands. The man was a dinosaur!

A woman came in and asked if there was a queue.

Yona nearly asked what for, before getting to the point and saying that there wasn't.

'It is rather hot, isn't it?' remarked the woman sympathetically as she went into the loo.

It was actually quite a cool day and Yona wondered briefly if the poor woman was deranged before catching sight of her flushed and furious face in the glass over the washbasin. Good grief, she looked as though she were approaching boiling point! She splashed her face with cold water before going to look for Meg and making her excuses for leaving early—and alone.

'Mike and I—we've had the most awful row,' she explained shakily, because only the truth would serve. 'So I've ordered a taxi. Time needed to cool down—you know how it is,' she wound up, acutely aware that Meg wouldn't really have any idea. It was unlikely that she and Ted had ever fought about anything.

'Go upstairs and wait in our room, dear, while I find Mike,' soothed Meg, proving that.

'No, no—it's serious, Meg. The end. He's going b-back to Fran.' Yona forced herself to spell it out, though she found the telling appalling. 'I'm sorry, Meg... Bless you. Thanks for everything...' Yona broke away, thrusting through the crowd and out of the house. She ran down the drive and stopped her taxi coming in.

Back home, she roamed restlessly about the flat, unable to keep still or think clearly. When the phone rang, she flew to it with fast-beating heart and surging hope, but it was Ted. 'Just checking that you got home all right,' he said gruffly.

'Oh...yes, thanks. Sorry I didn't see you before I—'

'No need, my dear—Meg has explained.'

'That's all right, then,' she responded, while thinking how absurd that sounded when everything was all wrong.

'If you want to come out here tomorrow, you'll be very welcome.'

'Thanks, Ted, I appreciate that, but I've promised to stand in for the chest registrar—some f-family thing.' His firstborn's christening, but it would have hurt too much to spell that out. Would she ever have a child of her own—now?

'You take on too much,' Ted was saying.

'I've never minded work, Ted.'

'Just so long as you remember there's more to life than work, Yona.'

How ironic that was after the day's events. 'Depends on the work,' she said, determined to keep her end up. 'See you on Monday, then—and thanks again...'

'You're welcome, dear girl,' said her boss as he hung up.

Yona resumed her restless prowling. How to put in the

rest of the day? Gil Salvesen had never forgiven her for standing him up and Nonie Burke had a new man. If only she'd been longer in Salchester, she'd know more people. Thank heaven she had a fortnight's holiday coming soon.

Yona hung up her new dress, took a bath and a sleeping pill and went to bed.

'I'm very sorry, Dr MacFarlane, but I can't find a vein,' said the new junior house officer, coming into the doctors' room.

'Dear me, that is serious,' murmured Yona, intent on the notes she was making. 'Have you asked Dr Price to take a look?'

'He's busy.'

And I can't be because I'm sitting down, thought Yona. Come back, Chris Connor, wherever you are. She'd lost count of the times this new boy had interrupted her this morning. 'I'll be done with this in three minutes and then I'll come and see. This is something I have to do for the prof—and it's urgent.'

'OK. I'd better take the tourniquet off, then, had I?'

'You mean you've—' Yona leapt up, scattering her precious notes, and shooed him ahead of her to the ward.

She needn't have worried. He hadn't put the thing on tight enough to constrict the blood flow, which was presumably why he hadn't been able to find a vein, as he'd put it.

'Why do we need blood from this lady now, anyway?' asked Yona in a low voice. 'I wrote her up for all the routine tests myself two days ago.'

'The lab rang and asked me. Apparently, most of it got spilt.'

'I see—well, there's no need to broadcast it. We don't want the patients thinking we're all careless,' hissed Yona out of the corner of her mouth as she reapplied the rubber tubing around the patient's biceps. When she felt the slight ballooning of the big vein on the front of the elbow joint, she deftly inserted the hypodermic needle and drew off the required amount of blood.

'I didn't want to constrict her too much in case I did any damage,' said young Dr Perkins when the procedure was over.

Even though he couldn't possibly have got this far without knowing it, Yona explained the difference between a tourniquet tight enough to stop the blood flow and control serious haemorrhaging and seconds of light pressure meant to produce a venous backlog sufficient to allow the removal of small quantities of blood for testing.

'Who actually told you to do this, anyway?' Yona asked when he'd insisted that he understood.

'Sister Evans. She said—'

'I can imagine what she said. Now, in future, if anybody other than Professor Burnley, Dr Price or myself, er, suggests that you do anything you're not sure about or haven't done before, you come straight to one of us three. Understand?'

'Oh, I've done that particular thing lots of times,' he said airily. 'Only that woman's got very difficult veins. A lot of people have, I find.'

'If you've done it lots of times, how come you didn't know to remove the tourniquet?' Yona asked keenly.

She had him there and he knew it. 'You may have qualified, Dr Perkins, but that's only the beginning,' Yona told him quietly but firmly. 'Please remember that.'

She went back to her interrupted work, but found she couldn't concentrate. That was the third time in as many days that she'd had occasion to reprimand him—and after the last time she'd overheard a sympathetic nurse explaining in a loud whisper that he mustn't mind poor Dr MacFarlane. She'd recently had a Big Disappointment and Sister says we must all Make Allowances for her!

Sister had been quite officiously kind this last week and Yona was finding that even harder to bear than her former hostility. So many of the hospital staff had been at the Burnleys' party that the whole hospital knew of her split with Mike scarcely twenty-four hours later.

Mike. Yona tried hard not to think of him, but he was always in her mind, refusing to be dismissed. She hadn't seen him since the day of the party and at first that had been a relief. Now it was an anxiety and a pain.

Once her initial anger and resentment had died down, Yona found herself hoping desperately that some time, somehow, things would work out for them, but each day that passed without so much as a glimpse of him made that increasingly unlikely. He had to be deliberately avoiding her—and that meant he'd accepted the break, even if she hadn't.

It could never have worked—you know fine it couldn't, she told herself for the millionth time as she gathered up all the papers and notes in the doctors' room and went to finish off in the peace and quiet of Ted's room in Outpatients.

She'd only just sat down at the desk when the door was flung open and she heard Mike exclaim, 'What the hell? Where's Ted?'

It was so close to the first thing he'd ever said to her in this very room on her first day that Yona almost cried out in pain. She fought back the emotion. 'Ted is at a one-day conference in Oxford,' she said quietly after a moment.

'So you're trying out the consultant's chair for size!'

Yona clenched her teeth. 'I'm sorting some facts and

figures Ted asked for—away from the distractions of the ward.'

'Here?'

She clenched her fists hard this time under cover of the desk, determined not to lose her poise. 'Why not? It's the obvious place. Most of the data I need is kept here and I have Ted's permission to use his room.'

'You never put a foot wrong, do you?' he asked with suppressed and baffled fury.

'What I always try to do is what my boss would want.'

'With an eye to the future.'

Any feelings of regret had been smothered by his cruel taunting. 'You bastard!' she exploded. 'Just because I don't conform to your antiquated ideas of the perfect woman, you can't allow me any virtues! Well, paint me as black as you like, if it's any comfort. I don't know what I ever saw in you! You're nothing but a selfish, puffed-up bully—and I hope I never see you again!'

A spasm of pain flashed across his face and was gone before she could be sure she'd actually seen it. Then he turned on his heel and left her without another word.

Yona put a shaking hand to her head, which was throbbing unbearably. She'd had too many of these heads since the break-up. All down to tension, of course, but she'd never imagined that a tension headache could be quite this bad.

She remembered hearing her father say once that if he could he'd prescribe the occasional backache or flu for all hospital workers—it would make them more sensitive to the sufferings of their patients. Wait till I get home, Dad, thought Yona, searching fruitlessly in her pocket for some aspirin. I'll tell you that the occasional tension headache would be quite sufficient!

Instead of going to lunch, Yona went to the pharmacy

to ask for some paracetamol. Having taken it, she lay down on the couch in Ted's room with the blinds down. She had a clinic that afternoon and by the time her first patient arrived she was feeling a bit better, but it was hours before the headache went away.

Over the next two weeks, Yona had too many more of those headaches, some of them severe enough to affect her vision. She hoped she wasn't starting with migraines—that was all a busy doctor needed. It was all down to stress, of course— though why had she started having queasiness as well? She couldn't remember feeling, let alone being, sick since she was a small child.

Two days before she was due to go on holiday, Yona realised that she'd missed a period. She had to sit down to take in the likeliest reason for that. But, no, it wasn't possible. She wasn't on the Pill, but Mike had always been so considerate. And yet...

She couldn't believe the joy flooding over her. It was crazy in the circumstances. Abortion was the sensible option, but she knew she couldn't, no matter what the difficulties and the cost—career-wise or any other way. She laid protective hands over her stomach, symbolically guarding her treasure.

'You've got another of your heads,' surmised Ted, coming into her consulting room and catching her staring into space with a dreamy, far-away look on her face.

She came back to the present and said, 'Only a mild one.'

'I've accepted your reluctance to consult a colleague here in the Royal,' said Ted, 'but will you promise me to see somebody when you get home? And another thing. You ought not to drive all that way alone, Yona. You must go by train.'

'All right—but only to please you, Ted. It's only tension, you know. I'll be fine when I've—when I've had a rest.'

'Perhaps, but young healthy women don't suddenly start getting headaches for no good reason, and you should know that.' He glanced at the pile of records on her desk. 'Though I must say that looks like enough to give anybody a headache—you've had a heavier clinic than I've had today. Away home with you now and put your feet up.' Then, just before leaving the room, he turned and said awkwardly, 'I hear that the Mellings, father and daughter, have gone off on a cruise. Nice for some.' Then he shambled out before Yona could say anything.

She found she didn't know what to make of that bit of news. She'd have expected Fran to stick to Mike like glue now she'd got him back. Then she realised that this holiday had probably been planned some time ago, before the doctor's accident—before the quarrel.

Mike was parking his car when Yona got home. It was only the second time she'd seen him since their break-up. She could see he meant to make a dash for it, but he was waylaid by the merry widow from the second floor and Yona arrived at the lifts just seconds before he did.

'You're early tonight,' she heard herself saying.

'It happens sometimes.' He pressed the button for the lift again before he asked, 'Aren't you supposed to be going on holiday soon?'

'Yes—right after work on Friday.'

'You'll be glad to be at home again, I suppose,' he said.

'Yes...it seems a long time since I was there.'

'About four months.'

'Four months and three days.' Oh, God! Was this what they had come to? Making awkward small talk, like the merest acquaintances meeting accidentally? Desperately

Yona raked her tired mind for something meaningful to say, but his lift came before she could come up with anything.

'Well, have a good rest,' said Mike. 'You look as though you could do with it.' Then he stepped in, the doors closed and he was gone.

Meg insisted on taking Yona to the station. 'Ted doesn't trust me not to fly,' said Yona when Meg came to the hospital to pick her up.

'You've got his number all right,' said Ted's devoted wife. 'Anyway, he's quite right, Yona. No driving and no flying until you're sorted out. I hope you've booked a seat.'

'I couldn't at such short notice so I'm going first class.'

'I do believe the girl's learning some sense at last,' returned Meg. 'Well, have a lovely time, dear—and come back fighting fit.'

Yona promised to do her best on that score, while wondering if she'd have the courage to come back at all in her condition. She still hadn't started her period.

To her astonishment and delight, her father was waiting for her at Edinburgh's Waverley station. He cast a clinical but fatherly eye over her and said, 'I'm glad you've got a man like Ted Burnley to keep an eye on you. He phoned me yesterday. He doesn't like these headaches you've been getting and neither do I so we'll be doing something about them while you're at home.'

It was useless to argue—Yona knew that. But what would they all think when they knew the rest? She meant to keep her precious secret as long as she could.

After a happy reunion with her family, followed by a restless night of apprehension, Yona found herself at Edinburgh's famous Royal Infirmary, being passed from consultant to consultant. It was first confirmed that she wasn't pregnant, and then she saw a neurologist first, then an endocrinologist and finally a chest specialist for good measure. What the blazes did they think was the matter with her? CAT scans, blood tests, X-rays and then, of all things, a skin biopsy for a Kveim test.

By then she'd tapped into their thinking and was ready for the verdict.

'There is a small pituitary tumour in the very early stages,' they told her. 'It's almost certainly benign and we're inclined to put it down to sarcoidosis—there are the typical changes apparent in the X-rays of your hands and feet. However, the Kveim test will confirm the diagnosis when we eventually get the result.' Yona knew there'd be a six-week waiting period for that.

'Headaches, vomiting, visual disturbances and increasing lassitude,' she summarised. 'I should have suspected something of the sort. Especially when my periods stopped—another symptom.' Against all reason Yona was ready to weep over not being pregnant.

'It's in the very early stages,' the consultant repeated, 'so we'll try high doses of steroids first—which is, after all, the treatment for sarcoid. Then radiotherapy if necessary and we'll only go for surgery as a last resort. It would be a pity to shave off any of that lovely hair.

'You'll have to stop work, of course, while you're on such high doses of prednisolone,' he continued, 'but then you'll know that already.'

Yona agreed, having seen that coming, and by the time she got home she knew exactly how she would be playing this. Her father wasn't home yet so she shut herself in his study to phone Ted.

He wasn't at all surprised to hear the diagnosis, but when she insisted on resigning he protested vigorously. 'I don't care how long you're off, your job will be here for you!'

he exclaimed. 'Dammit, girl, you're the best registrar I've ever had.'

'Bless you for that,' said Yona, feeling quite tearful at the tribute, 'but it has to be this way. Now that Mike and I— But I don't need to spell that out, do I? Please, Ted, you've got to promise me that you'll not tell him or anybody else the truth—barring dear Meg, of course.' She knew she couldn't bear it if Mike were to contact her out of pity.

'The story is this. I was homesick for Edinburgh and now I'm back home I don't intend to leave again. Is that clear?'

'You surely don't think anybody is going to believe that of a girl with your backbone, do you?' he demanded.

'People must believe what they choose, Ted. That is my story and I'm sticking to it. And you must admit that my way makes sense. You can't do without a registrar for any length of time, and this way you get to appoint a new one quickly. End of story. Do this for me as a friend, Ted—*please*! I'm begging you.'

It took a while longer, but she convinced him in the end. 'Not a word about my health now—to anybody,' she warned him finally.

'Well, if you're quite sure this is the way you want it, I guess I have to agree,' he said. 'But I shall phone every week to see how you are.'

'If I recover well enough for hospital work—and go on till I'm sixty—I'll never have a better boss than you, Ted Burnley,' said Yona, then she hung up.

It was the last day of September, and Yona was dozing in the garden of the MacFarlane family's holiday cottage on the Isle of Arran. They'd all agreed that this was the obvious place to bring her to convalesce once the initial arduous treatment was over and her dosage of steroids could begin to tail off gradually.

A bumble-bee, buzzing lazily inches from Yona's nose, woke her up. She looked up at the cloudless blue sky, then sideways at the little whitewashed cottage nestling into the gentle hillside. The cottage had been left to Mother by her granny, a native Arranach, and the whole family loved it dearly.

Yona sat up, the better to appreciate the magnificent panorama around her—the rolling hills, dotted with woodland and dying heather, the sparkling waters of Brodick Bay, the majestic mountains away to the north, dominated by Goat Fell, the highest yet the easiest to climb.

The family were climbing it on this perfect day. It was the first time they'd left her alone since they'd got here, and what a job she'd had persuading them that she'd be quite all right.

It had been good, though, always having somebody there for her. It stopped her thinking and wondering what was happening in Salchester. The Mellings would have got home from their cruise weeks ago…

With a muttered exclamation Yona hoisted herself off the lounger and strolled across the grass to lean on the low stone boundary wall and look down on the charming township of Brodick, strung out round the bay.

Down at the terminal the ferry was disgorging a seemingly never-ending stream of cars and lorries so it must be half past one. The ferry was always amazingly punctual, despite making the double crossing of the Firth of Clyde five times daily at this time of the year.

Yona supposed she ought to think about some lunch, but there was never any sense of haste in Arran—that was the secret of its peace. So she watched until the pride of the Caledonian MacBrayne fleet had taken on as many vehicles as it had brought and headed back towards its mainland port of Ardrossan. Then she wandered indoors at last to make a sandwich.

She had sliced and buttered some bread and was rummaging in the fridge for a filling when she heard steps on the gravel path, followed by a knock at the door. She shut the fridge and went to answer, thinking, The postie's very late today.

She opened the door and sagged against the lintel, gasping. It wasn't the postman but Mike standing there on the path, feet apart and looking determined. 'I had to come,' he said urgently. 'I couldn't stand it any longer...' His voice tailed off. It was his turn to stare now—at her once glorious hair, now thin and lustreless after all she'd been through. 'Oh, dear God, Yona,' he breathed. 'Whatever's the matter?'

'Ted broke his promise,' she said, because that was the only explanation. 'And I begged him not to tell.'

'Tell what? He doesn't know I'm here.'

'If he didn't tell you then why *are* you here—if it's not to pity me?'

He half reached towards her then dropped his hands in a gesture of despair. 'For God's sake, Yona, tell me what's wrong!' he pleaded in such obvious distress that she had to believe he knew nothing of her trouble.

She kept her explanation as brief as possible. 'I'd been getting headaches and they found a small benign tumour. Sarcoid,' she said over his gasp of horror. 'I've had radiotherapy and I'm on steroids and it's working.'

'You're not just saying that, are you? You really are on the mend?' he implored.

'Yes—there was barely a trace of it on the last scan.'

'Oh, thank God...' He pulled himself together and asked if he could come in.

'Yes, of course...' Yona turned and led the way into the homely sitting room. 'But why are you here? I mean, if you really didn't know?'

'It wasn't pity that brought me,' he said jerkily. 'It was sheer bloody misery! I had to see you—to try to—to put things right.'

'And you honestly didn't know I was ill?' She had to be absolutely sure about that.

'I didn't know. I thought you'd gone on holiday as planned. Then when you didn't come back and Ted got a locum in, he told us that you were on extended leave, taking stock. That made a sort of sense and I waited as patiently as I could...

'But when your job was finally advertised and he had to tell us you weren't coming back I felt as if I'd been poleaxed! If you didn't come back, how could we ever...? It took me several days to arrange to get away. I went straight to your parents' house in Edinburgh and found it all shut up. The next-door neighbour refused to tell me where you were so I went to the Southern General and got this address from your father's secretary—with the help of an orthopod I'd met once or twice.'

'You're very resourceful,' she remarked quietly, which wasn't easy with a heart rate that was now too fast to be counted.

'No—desperate,' he insisted. 'Quite desperate. I'd meant to try and talk you round when you came back, but when I heard you'd gone for good...I was *desperate*.

'You can make all the rules,' he said next. 'Do whatever you want—any way you want—I don't care. Just as long as you'll have me.' His voice was cracking. 'I can't live without you,' he whispered brokenly. 'And that's the truth.'

Despite her joy, she had to say, 'Look at me, Mike. No

hair to speak of and all plumped-up like a hamster with the steroids...'

But he was looking at her now with eyes so full of yearning that she felt dizzy with delight. 'I love you,' he said in a voice that shook with emotion. 'I love you. And if you don't love me—don't want me...' He turned his head sharply away so that she wouldn't see he was crying. 'I don't think I can go on. You're everything...' He could say no more.

Yona went to him and put her arms round him, and the feel of his lean hard body in her arms again was magic after all the weeks of sorrow and pain. 'I know,' she whispered. 'It's like that with me, too.'

They stood there a long time, holding one another ever closer. Then Mike said, 'I mean it, Yona. I'll never try to influence you again. The result was—just too terrifying.'

'You're such a dear, kind, good man,' she murmured. 'Always so fair and understanding in everything else. Why were you so determined to make me over into something I'm fairly sure I'm not?'

She thought he would never answer and then he said gently, 'You were so dedicated, so keen on your work—and so damn good at it! But I realise now the likeness ended there.'

'Likeness to whom, dearest?'

'My mother,' he said bleakly. 'She only ever came home to sleep, and left us altogether when I was fourteen. A highly paid job in London meant more to her than her son and her decent, hardworking but unambitious husband. I swore then that no child of mine would ever have to endure such a life!'

'I understand now,' she said softly. 'I just wish you'd told me sooner. Dear, I never believed I could have it all, but I did love my work and I needed to let go of it gradually, bit by bit—as family life required. Because you and our children would always, always be first with me. Listen now, I'm going to tell you something else...'

She stood on tiptoe to kiss him and rub her cheek against his and then she whispered in his ear about not understanding her symptoms and thinking she was pregnant.

'Pregnant!' he echoed. 'But why didn't you tell me?'

She'd guessed he'd say that. 'What—and put you under pressure. Never!'

'I know it's never been easier, but surely you didn't... Oh, Yona, tell me you didn't intend to—'

'Have a termination? No, I'd never have done that—never!' she cried passionately. 'It was crazy, irrational as things were, but I was glad about it, you hear? I was glad! And I'd have died before I'd have parted with our baby. And when I knew I wasn't pregnant and it was all down to the tumour, I felt cheated. Robbed. So now you know I'm not like your mother—don't you?' she ended.

'I certainly do—and I can't tell you how happy you've made me by sharing that with me. Now what's wrong?' he asked tenderly as her expressive face clouded over again.

'It's not certain, but there is just a chance...after the tumour and everything... I may not be able to...' She just couldn't say it.

Mike folded her close against his heart. 'If we have children, fine. If not, so be it. We've tried living without each other and that's just not on, is it?'

'It certainly is not,' she agreed fervently, as the crunch of several pairs of heavy boots on the gravel path announced the return of the MacFarlane clan.

'Is that my family back already?' She just couldn't believe it. 'I thought they'd be hours yet.'

Mike let her go in order to straighten his jacket and adjust his tie. 'Supposing they don't like me, Yona?' he asked apprehensively.

'Why wouldn't they? I do,' she said, smiling. 'Besides, in my delicate state of health they'd never want to upset me!'

He slid an arm around her waist again. 'I was right—you *are* a witch,' he was saying fondly as his future in-laws trooped in.

They took in the situation at a glance and came forward, smiling broadly.

MILLS & BOON®

Makes any time special

Enjoy a romantic novel from Mills & Boon®

Presents...   *Enchanted*   TEMPTATION.

Historical Romance™   **MEDICAL ROMANCE**

MILLS & BOON

MEDICAL ROMANCE

VETS AT CROSS PURPOSES by Mary Bowring

Rose Deakin's job in David Langley's practice was hard because of her ex-fiancé, for David didn't employ couples. And he thought Rose still cared for Pete.

A MILLENNIUM MIRACLE by Josie Metcalfe
Bundles of Joy

Kara had a wonderful wedding present for Mac—she was pregnant! But her joy turned to fear when a car smash put Mac in a life-threatening coma...

A CHANGE OF HEART by Alison Roberts
Bachelor Doctors

Lisa Kennedy seemed immune to David James—how could he convince her that he would happily give up his bachelor ways for her?

HEAVEN SENT by Carol Wood

Locum Dr Matt Carrig evoked responses in widowed GP Dr Abbie Ashby she hadn't felt in a long time. Could she risk her heart, when Matt seemed intent on returning to Australia?

Available from 7th January 2000

Available at most branches of WH Smith, Tesco, Martins, Borders, Easons, Volume One/James Thin and most good paperback bookshops

MILLS & BOON®

SPECIAL PRICE £3.50

Coming in January 2000...

ACCIDENT AND EMERGENCY

Three exciting stories based in the casualty departments of busy hospitals. Meet the staff who juggle an active career and still find time for romance and the patients who depend on their care to reach a full recovery.

Three of your favourite authors:

Caroline Anderson
Josie Metcalfe
Sharon Kendrick

Available at most branches of WH Smith, Tesco, Martins, Borders, Easons, Volume One/James Thin and most good paperback bookshops

MILLS & BOON®

MISTLETOE *Magic*

Three favourite Enchanted™ authors bring you romance at Christmas.

Three stories in one volume:

A Christmas Romance
BETTY NEELS

Outback Christmas
MARGARET WAY

Sarah's First Christmas
REBECCA WINTERS

Published 19th November 1999

Available at most branches of WH Smith, Tesco, Martins, Borders, Easons, Volume One/James Thin and most good paperback bookshops

10...9...8...

As the clock struck midnight three single people became instant parents...

Millennium baby

Kristine Rolofson
Baby, It's Cold Outside

Bobby Hutchinson
One-Night-Stand Baby

Judith Arnold
Baby Jane Doe

Celebrate the Millennium with these three heart-warming stories of instant parenthood

Available from 24th December

FREE
2 BOOKS
AND A SURPRISE GIFT!

We would like to take this opportunity to thank you for reading this Mills & Boon® book by offering you the chance to take TWO more specially selected titles from the Medical Romance™ series absolutely FREE! We're also making this offer to introduce you to the benefits of the Reader Service™ —

- ★ FREE home delivery
- ★ FREE monthly Newsletter
- ★ FREE gifts and competitions
- ★ Exclusive Reader Service discounts
- ★ Books available before they're in the shops

Accepting these FREE books and gift places you under no obligation to buy; you may cancel at any time, even after receiving your free shipment. Simply complete your details below and return the entire page to the address below. **You don't even need a stamp!**

YES! Please send me 2 free Medical Romance books and a surprise gift. I understand that unless you hear from me, I will receive 4 superb new titles every month for just £2.40 each, postage and packing free. I am under no obligation to purchase any books and may cancel my subscription at any time. The free books and gift will be mine to keep in any case.

M9EC

Ms/Mrs/Miss/Mr .... Initials ....
BLOCK CAPITALS PLEASE
Surname ....
Address ....
....
.... Postcode ....

Send this whole page to:
UK: FREEPOST CN81, Croydon, CR9 3WZ
EIRE: PO Box 4546, Kilcock, County Kildare (stamp required)

Offer valid in UK and Eire only and not available to current Reader Service subscribers to this series. We reserve the right to refuse an application and applicants must be aged 18 years or over. Only one application per household. Terms and prices subject to change without notice. Offer expires 30th June 2000. As a result of this application, you may receive further offers from Harlequin Mills & Boon Limited and other carefully selected companies. If you would prefer not to share in this opportunity please write to The Data Manager at the address above.

Mills & Boon is a registered trademark owned by Harlequin Mills & Boon Limited.
Medical Romance is being used as a trademark.

MILLS & BOON®
Makes any time special™

By Request

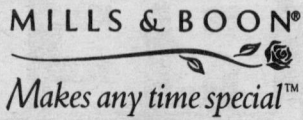

Bestselling themed romances brought back to you by popular demand

Each month By Request brings you three full-length novels in one beautiful volume featuring the best of the best.

So if you missed a favourite Romance the first time around, here is your chance to relive the magic from some of our most popular authors.

Look out for

Christmas Presents

in December 1999

featuring Penny Jordan, Anne McAllister and Sally Wentworth

Available at most branches of WH Smith, Tesco, Martins, Borders, Easons, Volume One/James Thin and most good paperback bookshops